Clink! Rapper froze. Where did that sound come from?

Slowly, he took one step forward, toward the closest mound of trash. Step-by-silent-step, he made his way around the pile.

Crunch. Rapper heard the footstep. Only...*funny*...it wasn't coming from in front of him, but—

Rapper whirled around and came face to face with a Viper gang member. Both Rapper and the Viper jumped back, startled. Then without a moment's notice, the Viper took off. On instinct, Rapper took off after him, leaping over puddles. He held the knife at his side as he pursued. Rapper knew most Vipers only carried one knife...and Rapper must have had this Viper's only knife or he would have swiped first and asked questions later.

"Stop!" Rapper cried. "I just want to talk to you!"

The Viper continued. et out an ear-piercing whistle le came from nearby. Ten mo d each other. They headed for

"Stop!" Rapp They weren't listening.

Ahead, the chained dogs barked furiously.

A scream! The second Viper tripped and fell face first to the ground. Underneath him, gravel and mud spurted out like a stifled firework.

Rapper immediately stopped in his tracks...but not because the Viper fell. Rapper stopped because the scream was...a female scream. In the rain, Rapper blinked. *Since when did Vipers allow girls in the gang?* Adrenaline flowing through him, Rapper pulled the knife out of the belt loop of his overalls. He approached the fallen Viper.

"Don't move!" he shouted.

Look for these other books in the
Commander Kellie and the Superkids~SM~ **Series!**

*Commander Kellie and the Superkids*_{SM}

#6

Mystery of the Missing Junk

Christopher P.N. Maselli

Harrison House
Tulsa, Oklahoma

10 09 08 07 06 05 04 03 02 01   10 9 8 7 6 5 4 3 2 1

This book is a work of fiction. Names, characters, places and incidents in this adventure are products of the author's imagination or are used fictitiously. Any resemblance to actual events or locales or people, living or dead, is entirely coincidental.

Based on the characters created by Kellie Copeland, Win Kutz, Susan Wehlacz and Loren Johnson.

Mystery of the Missing Junk
ISBN 1-57794-232-9   KC-30-0906
Copyright © 2001 by Kenneth Copeland Ministries
Fort Worth, Texas 76192-0001

Published by Harrison House, Inc.
P.O. Box 35035
Tulsa, Oklahoma 74153

Dedication

To Missy "the driving force" Johnson for her unending support, her enduring pursuit of excellence, and for seeing the treasure in all my creative junk.

Contents

Yo Superkid!

Hey—I'm Rapper Rapfield and I was just dropped into a mystery that kept me guessing until the end! Finding the truth, I discovered, was a bigger challenge than I had anticipated...or hoped.

Let me rewind a sec and tell you a bit about me. I'm a Superkid and I live at Superkid Academy. I've been there about four years now, training with the Blue Squad. With them, it's one adventure after another.

There are five of us in the Blue Squad—me, Paul, Missy, Valerie and Alex. And our leader is Commander Kellie—she's someone I can always count on. She's the one who has taught me about the power of God's Word and showed me how rad it is to have a relationship with Jesus.

I'm glad she showed me those things, too...because when I was slam-dunked into this adventure, little did I know the truths she taught me would be challenged to the hilt. If I hadn't been sure about the fact that life with God is the only real life there is, I might never have pressed through to the answer. And then I'd have never discovered the truth. So, check it out. Maybe you can figure it out sooner than I did!

Rapper

Mystery of the Missing Junk

Rapper could already tell that free falling was not his cup of tea. Of course, it didn't help that he was blindfolded and his arms were bound behind his back. That is why, as he fell head over heels, his legs kicking in the open air, he screamed.

"Aaaaaaaaaaagggggggghhhhhhhh!!!!!!!!!!!!!!!!!!!!"

It didn't do much good.

"Help me Jesus! Help me Jesus! Help me Jesus!" he cried.

Rapper figured this is what he got for picking a fight several hundred feet in the air, on an open Serfsled. The flying vehicle was shaped somewhat like a vintage motorcycle with an oval plate on the bottom to keep it steady. Rapper had been seated on the back, and had started the fight when he started smarting off to his captor. This, he calculated, had not been his best strategy.

It had all begun several hours ago when the Superkid was captured by Mashela Knavery—a fugitive who had one thing on her mind: getting away fast. Weeks prior, *she* had been captured by Superkid Academy. But then she escaped with Rapper as her insurance—but not before being temporarily blinded by a blast of light his commander had shot at her. At least now Mashela would never know the secret location of Superkid Academy.

Rapper knew that his commander, Commander Kellie at Superkid Academy, would do everything she could to rescue him. And he knew his best friends on the Blue Squad—Paul, Missy, Valerie and Alex—would be right there with her. But somehow, Mashela had managed to evade them all. And Rapper was alone. And Mashela was not exactly ideal company. That's why the 12-year-old Superkid decided to do *something* to change his situation as they sped through the air. So, Rapper kicked her in the ankle. Now, as he fell through the open air, he deeply regretted the move, imagining the newspaper story:

SUPERKID KISSES GROUND WHILE TRAVELING AT HIGH SPEED

Superkid Robert "Rapper" Rapfield plummeted to the earth yesterday, reportedly after diving off an open vehicle. When asked what happened, Rapfield said, "Ehhhhhhhhhh...Mommy?" Further interviews will be conducted in five years, when he'll be sawed out of his full-body cast.

In the distance, Rapper could hear her laughing. He could see her in his mind: beautiful, dark-skinned, curly black hair—laughing at him. She was coldhearted, ruthless, merciless...but not hopeless. Each of the

Superkids had seen it—she had a soft side. She was an agent of NME, but not necessarily by choice. NME had taken her from an orphanage at a young age. Since then, the dark organization was all she had known.

NME was an organization pitted against the Superkids—because the Superkids were committed to spreading the message of Jesus...the message of truth. NME wanted to turn the world's children into *their* followers. They wanted kids to live in fear of them so they would be forced to do their dirty deeds. But the Superkids knew there was a way to break NME's grasp of fear: by shining the light of the truth—God's Word.

That Word had touched Mashela, Rapper was sure of it. Sure, she'd broken out of confinement. Sure, she had just smacked him in the mouth with the back of her hand. Sure, he was now cascading down to earth, perhaps to his demise, because of her. Still, Rapper was sure she had been touched by the Truth. Now, she sailed on, an infidel. She was too proud to go back to NME... besides, they'd probably want her head for being caught. And she was too hardhearted to let the Superkids know she respected their Truth. She would probably go it alone for a while, Rapper thought. For now, he would pray for her. As the Superkid Manual says in Ephesians 6:12, his struggle was not against flesh and blood—people like Mashela—but against the spiritual rulers and authorities and powers of this world's darkness.

This and many other thoughts and prayers zipped through Rapper's mind in the seconds he spun through the open air like a kamikaze airplane. Meanwhile, his mouth was still busy screaming. Until finally...

CRRRRRRAAAAASSSSSSSHHHHHHHH!!!!!!!!!!!!!!!!!

Bam! Boom! Smash! Crash! Still blindfolded and bound, Rapper wasn't sure what he'd hit with a belly-flop, but best he could tell, it was a thick pile of old mattresses. The pain of impact shot through him, but not drastically. It sure felt like a long fall, but perhaps they hadn't been as high as he'd thought.

Rapper's body bounced up and off the pile, rolling down a hill of bumpy objects. He could hear the scraping of metal, the cracking of plastic and the shattering of glass. His nose was the first to inform him that he had surely plummeted into a junkyard.

"Thank You, Jesus," he said aloud, knowing full well the Lord had protected his fall. He could tell he would have several bruises, but otherwise he felt all right. A headache was begging to come on, but Rapper pushed it aside by setting his mind on the Word. "I am healed by Jesus' wounds," he said, remembering 1 Peter 2:24.

Time and again, the Lord had protected the Superkid, and this was no exception. Protection was just one of the promises he had in his relationship with God. Rapper was thankful he had made Jesus his Lord at an early age...and learned what it was like to have a real, living relationship with Him.

Rapper sat up among the trash, listening for the soft swoosh of the Serfsled. He heard machinery and crunching metal, but he didn't hear the Serfsled. He wasn't surprised. Mashela was surely long gone by now. Boy, he couldn't wait to see her again. How he wanted to show her he was all right—yes, her little plan to get rid of him failed. He was all right! "Whooo-hooo!" Rapper shouted.

Now if he could just find out where he was...

Cautiously, Rapper leaned back and rolled the back of his head against the nearest protrusion. As he did, the blindfold slowly pulled up, allowing him to see. Rapper's eyelids shut tight as the late afternoon sun pierced his brown eyes. He blinked the spots away and looked around him.

Piles of trash—each 10 to 15 feet high—surrounded him like awkward, miniature mountains. The clay ground between the mountains was brown and lumpy. Rapper couldn't see any working machines from where he sat, although he could hear them buzzing nearby. After a long breath, Rapper leaned forward onto his knees and then pushed himself up with his calves. His legs felt like gelatin. Rapper shook his body, trying to free himself from a large, metal hovercar bumper that had twisted around his stomach. It wouldn't budge. He pulled at the thick, silver, duct tape around his wrists, but couldn't break it.

Hmmmmmmmmm...

Rapper heard the vibration fill the area, but he couldn't tell where it was coming from. Had Mashela returned on the Serfsled?

Then Rapper looked up.

His eyes grew saucer-sized as a wide, silver disc hovered 20 feet above him. Rapper gulped.

FOOOOOOM!

With astounding power, the disc powered on and a clump of metal trash under the disc shot straight up. Of course, since Rapper was under the disc and had a metal bumper wrapped around his midsection, he went straight up, too.

"Whoa!" Rapper shouted, lifting into the air. At once, the metal bumper around him clung to the disc like a magnet. At first Rapper struggled to break free, but then reconsidered; he was high enough that he didn't want to fall—again.

From up in the air, Rapper could clearly see the layout of the junkyard. Half the yard was covered with small mountains of junk, evenly spaced and equally high. To the east lay a small, metal building—probably an office of some sort—just past an active conveyor belt and two small, occupied booths. Farther to the north, near the front gate, was a small bi-level, wooden dwelling. Black, chain-link fence surrounded the yard. Topping it off were three red lines of thin, glowing laser beams. If Rapper didn't know better, he would have thought he'd dropped into a top-secret military complex. Past the fence, plains rolled toward a city, many miles away. Rapper could faintly see the city skyline in the distance.

Slowly, Rapper sailed through the air with a lump of trash, scurried along by the magnetic disc. He figured one of the occupants in the small booths ahead must be controlling the disc, completely oblivious to Rapper's sudden attachment.

"Hello-o-o!" Rapper shouted, but no one heard him. He looked around the sky for any indication of Mashela. She was long gone.

Fooomp!

Rapper heard the electromagnet shut off. Suddenly, he was free falling again, his stomach leaping into his throat.

"Aaaagggggghhhhh!" he shouted.

Whump! Rapper hit the active conveyer belt and was suddenly being pulled along with his and other mounds of junk.

"Hey!" Rapper turned his head to see the man in the first small booth stand up. His dark-skinned, bald head was accented by a black goatee and black eyes. Denim overalls and a plaid, flannel shirt covered his hefty build. "There's a kid on the belt!" he shouted.

The man in the other booth, light-skinned and scrawny, just formed an "O" with his mouth. His brown hair looked like a mess of twigs.

"Could be our thief!" the big man shouted to his twig-headed co-worker.

A short distance away, at the bi-level dwelling, a window shot up and a young, dark-skinned girl peered out. She glared at Rapper and then slammed down the window.

Rapper looked up the conveyor belt and saw the trash disappear into a canopied tunnel ahead. Every time a piece entered, a deep, crunching sound echoed from the abyss. Rapper wasn't sure what the machine was, but he did know one thing—he had to get off!

Crunch.

Rapper tried rolling off the belt, but couldn't gain momentum with the bumper around his waist.

Crunch!

The end was still about 25 feet away. Rapper fidgeted as he bent his head around to look at the junk surrounding him. There! Very close to his hands was a thick plastic container with a jagged edge. He shuffled over to it. "No weapon formed against me will prevail," he said, quoting Isaiah 54:17.

Crunch!!

Quickly, but carefully, Rapper sawed his duct tape binds on the edge of the container. "This isn't as easy as it should be/gotta cut through if I wanna get free!" Rapper rapped. He always rapped when he was nervous.

CRUNCH!!

Rapper was close enough to the canopied tunnel ahead that the crunching sounded like a lion's roar.

Snap! Rapper broke free—not a second too soon. He pushed himself up. He leapt off the conveyor belt and hit the ground.

"Thank You, Jesus," he said aloud. He ran his hands through his spiked, brown hair. He rubbed his wrists. Then he gulped. Three junk mounds down he saw them darting toward him: two big, black, junkyard dogs.

"Heh-heh, nice doggies," he whimpered. At once he took off down another aisle, hoping to lose the dogs between mounds. No good. The dogs, baring their teeth and barking, tracked him quickly. They sent him climbing clumsily up the nearest mountain.

"The Lord is faithful—He will strengthen and protect me!" Rapper shouted 2 Thessalonians 3:3. Even in the toughest times, Rapper's first thoughts went to the Lord—God had always been faithful to Rapper.

"Woof! Woof! Woof!" the dogs barked angrily back, proud to have caught their intruder. Rapper's foot slipped and one of the dogs snapped at him. He pulled his foot away fast.

Rapper carefully leaned forward and could see one of the booths in the distance. The large, bald man was looking at him and chuckling.

"Hey!" Rapper shouted, "Could I get a little help here?!"

"Woof! Woof!" the dogs yapped.

Rapper was about to command the dogs to be quiet in Jesus' Name when suddenly standing before him was the girl he'd seen peek out the window. She was about

12 years old, Rapper guessed, medium-height and had a sure stance. Her dark skin accented her deep brown eyes, which sparkled as the sun hit them. They became deeper as the sun crept behind a dark cloud.

Her cheekbones weren't high, her lips were thin, her face was round and her curly, black hair was shaved up in the back. She had some kind of wispy-style thing happening on the top. Rapper was sure his friend Missy knew the proper name for the style. The girl was wearing simple clothes: an orange sweat shirt, jeans and athletic shoes.

Shortly, she had the dogs calmed down, but she didn't send them away. They stood on either side of her, still growling at Rapper.

"So I guess we've finally caught our thief, haven't we?" she accused.

"Huh?" Rapper asked. "Uh, no, I just ended up in the wrong place at the wrong time..." He pulled at the hovercar bumper around his waist. "Next thing I know, Lassie's mean cousins are after me."

"You mind calling them off?" he added.

"What are you doing here?" the girl demanded. "You're trying to steal autocomms aren't you?"

Rapper had heard of autocomms. They were small units placed in hovercars that allowed communication over great distances. They were expensive, which is why most mechanics bought used autocomms at junkyards when replacing defective ones.

"Autocomms?" Rapper asked the girl. "Someone's stealing autocomms from you? Who?!"

"I think *you're* stealing autocomms from us," the girl accused. "Admit it."

"I'm not—look, can I use your ComPhone? I need to get hold of someone to pick me up. Where am I anyway?"

The girl twisted her lip, staring at him as if she were thinking, *Sure, play dumb.*

Rapper started to step down, but one of the dogs growled at him again. Rapper retracted his foot. "Look," he said, finally prying off the bumper around his waist. "I'm filthy and I just want to go home. I didn't steal any autocomms. You can search me if you want, but you won't find anything."

"That's some get-up," the girl said after a pause. She nodded at his clothing.

Rapper brushed off his sleeve. After landing in the junk pile and riding the conveyor belt, his royal blue uniform was filthy. He wiped a smudge off the Superkid wings pin on the left side of his chest.

"It's a Superkid uniform," Rapper explained. "Though it's rather dirty," he sniffed it, "and smelly now."

"Y-you're a Superkid?" the girl stammered.

Rapper nodded.

"Hey, Karla!" the big man in the booth hollered down the aisle. He leaned out. "What's going on? Who is that? Need me to get your dad?"

Karla snapped out of her gaze at Rapper and waved her hand at the man.

"Uh, no!" she shouted back. "It's just one of my friends—dropped in! No prob!"

"Well tell him to keep off the belts," he stated with a shrug and then sat back down. He resumed fiddling with the controls.

The wind kicked up a bit. Karla turned to Rapper.

"You're really a Superkid?" she asked again. Rapper looked at her brown eyes and saw the wonderment in them. Or was it...expectation?

"I really don't want to cause any trouble," Rapper offered. "If I could just use a ComPhone..."

"You a Christian?" Karla asked. She hadn't taken her eyes off him.

"Yes," he said solemnly, but sure.

Karla let out a long breath and looked around the yard. "You have to change. *Fast.* I'll get your uniform washed for you."

Rapper nodded and smiled. Finally, some help. The Lord was always faithful to His Word. "That would be great. You know I didn't steal the autocomms then?"

A warm smile pushed up Karla's thin lips at the edges. "Yes, I know you didn't steal the autocomms."

"Good," Rapper said, letting out a deep breath. "Then would you mind calling off the dogs?"

What Rapper couldn't figure out was why Karla wanted him to change *fast*. He was more than happy to change out of the filthy uniform, but Karla seemed very adamant about it...as if she had an ulterior motive in getting him to change. Rapper shook it off. Maybe he was just being overly suspicious. After all, at least he'd found someone to help. And she was nice, too!

Karla's house was, as he had seen from above the junkyard, a bi-level dwelling. The living quarters were on the second level, with only a garage and storage area underneath. It was long and flat, not flashy, but not trashy, either. The structure was made of wood and aluminum siding, painted tan with dark-brown trim. To get inside, Karla led Rapper up a winding series of wooden plank steps to the front door. Sliding windows were on either side.

Inside, she led him through a quaint living room with gray carpet, past a tiny kitchen. She left him in a square room with an antique-looking daybed and matching dresser. Her own room was 10 steps down the hall, she said, by the bathroom, and her dad's bedroom was in the other direction. After Rapper changed, she promised to take his clothes down to the laundry room by the garage and give them a spin.

Rapper thanked her, blindly accepting some temporary threads, and closed the door.

▲ ▲ ▲

Rapper exited his room and rubbed his temples with the forefinger and thumb of one hand. Karla met him in the hall, closing her bedroom door behind her. Rapper handed her his dirty, royal blue uniform and smiled.

"Are you sure this is all you have for me to wear?" he asked, looking down at the new clothes he wore.

Karla smiled back. "It's all I have that will fit you that's not a dress and that I don't have to go digging for, yes," she said. "Don't look a gift horse in the mouth."

Rapper shook his head. "It's not that. It's just that...overalls are usually not my style."

Karla thumped him on the chest with a fist. "Don't worry. No one will even notice," she said, marching forward. Rapper was sure he heard her giggle. He followed her.

As they made their way down the hall to the kitchen, Rapper heard the electronic sliding of the front door, followed by some gruff voices. At once, Karla folded his uniform into an indistinguishable blue ball of fabric. She whispered a quick message over her shoulder, "Nothing about being a Superkid, OK?"

Rapper nodded, not sure why she would say that. He made a mental note to ask her later.

As they entered the living room, Rapper realized he fit right in. The plump, bald man and the scrawny man he had seen earlier in the operations booths were both in shirts and overalls. The third man, obviously the one in charge, was also in overalls. He had a thick build, snowy hair and a stern face. His nose was flat and his eyes dark. His skin was the same dark-brown tone as Karla's and Rapper guessed he was somehow related to her.

"...movin' right along," he was saying to the other two gentlemen. "We should meet our quota by the end of the month."

"If not beat it," the big man added.

"'Less it all gets stolen," the lanky man drawled. The other two men nodded.

The big man was the first to see Rapper. He chuckled and pointed at him. "We thought we caught the thief today—there he is!" he said.

The group turned and the eyebrows of the man in charge bobbed up. "So you're the one causing us trouble, huh?"

"Uh, I don't mean to be any—"

The man in charge interrupted Rapper's apology. "Ain't no trouble," he said with a chuckle. "We were just hoping to nail down our robber." He turned to the lanky man with the twiggy hair. "What's it been? Four years?"

The lanky man shrugged. Slowly he said, "Maybe five."

"Someone's been robbing you for five years?" Rapper questioned. Everyone nodded. "They stole a lot?" he asked.

"They've stolen too much," the man in charge said plainly.

The room fell silent for a moment. Rapper recognized their expressions too well. It was more than five years ago when the devil worked his worst to steal from Rapper and his family. Rapper's dad left the family—Rapper still didn't understand why. And that's when the money and the comforts left, too.

Rapper's brother, Nick, couldn't handle it. Before long, he joined a gang called the Vipers, looking for the love he was missing at home. Soon after, Rapper was hanging out with the gang, too. Then it happened. Rapper's brother was shot one night by a rival gang member. His life was stolen right there on the spot...and it changed Rapper forever.

Commander Kellie and Superkid Academy came along soon after that incident...and Rapper was eager to join them. He knew his mom still needed time to heal...and he needed to get as far as he could from the Vipers. Since then, Rapper and his mom had grown much closer as the Lord healed their wounds. Even Rapper's dad seemed to be coming around—despite the fact that Rapper only saw him on an occasional holiday. One thing was for sure: Rapper wasn't about to give the devil any inroad to messing with his life again. John 10:10

says Satan comes to kill, steal and destroy—but Jesus came to give life in its fullest. And Rapper wasn't about to let go of his life in God, no matter what the cost.

The man in charge stretched out his hand. "I'm Karla's dad, Kentren Fenwood III," he said. It struck a chord with Rapper—*Where had he heard that name before?* Mr. Fenwood added, "This is Buddy and that's Zeke." Buddy was the big, bald man, Zeke the lanky.

"I'm Rapper Rapfield," Rapper said. "I just—"

"He's a friend from school," Karla interrupted. "Just came by to mess around."

"Looks like you'll fit right in," Mr. Fenwood said with a nod. Rapper looked down at his overalls and let out a short breath.

"Well, I'm glad," Mr. Fenwood said to his daughter. "'Bout time you made some good friends. Maybe now you'll sleep better." His gaze turned to Rapper. "She's always sluggish in the mornin'."

"Everyone's sluggish in the morning," Karla said defensively.

"Sometimes I'm sluggish in the mornin's," Zeke drawled.

Buddy chuckled. "You're always sluggish," he added. Zeke pursed his lips in protest.

"You going to make dinner, Hun?" Mr. Fenwood asked his daughter.

She nodded. "OK." She turned to Rapper. "You like hot dogs and beans?"

Rapper put his arms out. "Well, I'm dressed for it—but I don't want to intrude."

"No—please," Karla insisted rather abruptly, "stay for dinner."

Rapper looked into Karla's eyes. What was she hiding? Was something wrong? He couldn't tell. Everything seemed all right on the surface, but Rapper couldn't help but wonder.

"Yeah, join us," Mr. Fenwood said. "It's not often we get company way out here. In fact, why not stay overnight? Just call your parents and let 'em know. We have an extra bedroom and then you can just ride into school tomorrow on the bus with Karla."

"Well, actually," Rapper said, "I—"

"Sounds great!" Karla said, with a thump on his balled-up uniform. She grabbed his arm. "Let's go make dinner!"

In a flash, Karla rushed Rapper out of the room and into the small kitchen. It was a rather plain room—off-white with no decorations.

Karla let go of Rapper's arm, set his uniform by the back door and started digging through a cupboard, recovering a couple cans of beans.

Rapper wasn't the kind of person to get suspicious, but he thought Karla's behavior was rather strange. What was this all about? Why was she insisting he stay for dinner...and now the night? Rapper was about to ask point-blank, but thought better of it. The Holy Spirit wasn't alerting him to any danger, so he decided to play along. Besides, the "detective" part of Rapper wanted to figure out who it was that was stealing autocomms from the junkyard.

As he listened to the men talking about this and that in the other room, he couldn't help but wonder, *What if it's Buddy or Zeke? Or both of them?* It had to be someone familiar with the junkyard—especially if they've been able to pull the wool over Mr. Fenwood's eyes for five years. *But what would be their motivation?* Then Rapper wondered, *Could Karla's insistence that I stay be tied to the robberies?*

"Hey, Karla?" Rapper asked. Karla turned toward him while breaking open a hot dog pack. "You mind if I use the ComPhone now?"

▲ ▲ ▲

In a nook in the kitchen, Rapper dialed the number for Superkid Academy. He input his secret access code and was routed directly to the main control center. He was staring at a blank screen when suddenly his friend Alex's face popped up on it. Upon seeing Rapper, he choked on his words, then screamed. Rapper jumped back and turned down the volume on the ComPhone.

"You're not dead!" Alex shouted. "You're not dead!" He turned around on screen. "He's not dead! Commander Kellie! Rapper's not dead!"

"You thought I was *dead?!*" Rapper asked.

Alex turned back around. His jaw dropped and then he pulled it up into a smile. "Did I say dead? Uh, no—I meant *red* from *sunburn.* You're not red! Whoo-hoo!"

Rapper wasn't convinced. "Thanks, Alex," he offered flatly, "for being happy that I'm not *red.*"

"Heh-heh."

"Heh-heh."

Commander Kellie's face replaced Alex's. "Praise God! Rapper, are you all right?" she greeted. "Where are you?"

Rapper bit his bottom lip. It was good to see his commander again. She looked dignified, as usual. Her straight, dark-brown hair cupped down around her face. Her brown eyes flashed with a confidence in the Lord Rapper hoped would one day be equally reflected in his own eyes. "Wow. Good question. I haven't even asked where I am. But I'm all right."

"Are you safe?"

"Yeah, I'm really fine," Rapper explained. "I thought Mashela was going to take me somewhere in particular, but I guess not. We were flying for a few hours, I think. The next thing I know, we got in a fight, she released my seat belt and knocked me off the Serfsled."

"In mid-flight?!" Commander Kellie asked, her voice full of concern. "How high were you?"

"I dunno," Rapper replied. "I was still blindfolded when I fell. But I landed in a junkyard. Mashela kept going."

"The Lord protected you, Rapper—just like Psalm 91 promises He will. We've been praying nearly nonstop since you were kidnapped. The Lord's angels have been keeping charge over you. We'd have come after you, but somehow Mashela blew out our main power grid. She essentially locked us in our own building. Anyway, we'd just gotten things back in order when you called."

After a brief pause, Rapper lowered his voice and explained to his commander everything else that had happened: Karla's insistence that he stay, the familiar name of the father, the fact that someone had been stealing from their junkyard—for five years, no less.

"All right," Commander Kellie submitted, "if you feel this is something the Lord wants you to check out a bit more, that's fine. We'll run the father's name through the Academy computer and see if anything comes up. We can just come get you tomorrow after you ride into the nearest town with Karla."

"I do think there is something the Lord wants me to do here," Rapper stated surely. "I don't think it's an accident I'm here." Rapper wanted to solve the mystery, but he also wanted to share God's promises with the Fenwoods so they could stand against the enemy.

"Thanks, Commander," Rapper said. "I'll call you from town tomorrow."

Commander Kellie smiled warmly and signed off. Rapper pressed the "Disconnect" button and scratched his head.

Father, he prayed silently, *show me Your wisdom according to James 1:5. Prosper my mind as I do Your will. May the words of my mouth and the meditation of my heart be pleasing in Your sight—Psalm 19:14. May my actions glorify You. In Jesus' Name, Amen.*

▲   ▲   ▲

"Everything OK?" Karla asked. She was standing at the stove, selecting the heat ratio, turn speed and grill pattern for the hot dogs. Short beeps came from the unit.

"Everything's great!" Rapper said. "I'll just ride into town with you tomorrow. Anything I can help with?"

"Dog food's in the pantry," Karla said, nodding toward two large dog dishes on the floor. Rapper took the hint and filled up the dishes.

"How long have you guys lived here?" Rapper asked.

Karla shrugged. "Well, I'm 12, so I guess 12 years."

Rapper picked up the dog dishes and set them by the back door. "I'll just put these over here so your dad can take them out. I don't think the dogs like me."

"The dogs don't like *anyone,*" Karla said with a smirk. "They won't even let *him* get too close."

"They didn't seem to mind you," Rapper noted.

"Whoo-whee," Karla shot back, twirling her finger in the air. "So I get blessed with being the official dog feeder."

"What about your mom?" Rapper asked.

Karla froze for a second, then moved on as if Rapper hadn't asked a question. He waited, but nothing ever came.

Rapper thought about asking again, but decided against it. It was just another puzzle piece to figuring out this strange family. *Thank You for Your wisdom, Lord,* Rapper prayed James 1:5 silently again.

"So," Rapper tried another subject, "are you a Christian?"

Karla froze for a second again. He was obviously making her uncomfortable.

"I was just wondering," he explained, "because if you are, there are certain promises God has given you that you can stand on. You don't have to put up with the devil robbing you. Colossians 2:6 says just as you trusted Christ to save you, you can trust Him, too, for each day's problems. That's part of living in union with Him and His Word. If you resist the devil and stand firm in faith—"

Mr. Fenwood suddenly walked into the kitchen, his work boots clomping on the floor. "Guys are gone," he stated. "Looks like it's gonna rain tonight. I locked up the front. You chain the dogs yet?" he asked Karla.

Karla nodded. Apparently her and Rapper's conversation was over.

"Buddy said he'd set the alarm at the front gate." He swung out a chair and sat down in it backward.

"You have an alarm system and stuff is still getting robbed?" Rapper asked.

"They're good," Mr. Fenwood admitted. "We haven't found anything to stop 'em yet."

Rapper couldn't help but suggest it. "Maybe they have the code to the alarm."

Mr. Fenwood rubbed his eyes and yawned. "Only Karla and I have the code."

"And Buddy," Rapper added.

Karla shot a glance at Rapper. Mr. Fenwood placed his hands on the kitchen table, over the back of the chair. He looked at Rapper, too.

"Yes, and Buddy. And Zeke. What? You think one of them's been stealing from me for five years?" He chuckled. "No judgment here, but quite honestly, those boys ain't smart enough to do much more than run the machines. I doubt they're involved in a master plot to steal from me."

"So what's being stolen?" Rapper asked. "Just autocomms?"

"That's enough," Karla's dad said. "Autocomms alone could support our business year 'round. They're a popular commodity. That's why statistically they're *número uno* on the national stolen items report."

Rapper thought about Mr. Fenwood's words as he sauntered over to the back door and looked out. The clouds had darkened the sky considerably and the sun was nearly down. Tiny, light, rain droplets popped onto the window. Rapper squinted into the yard. Nothing much was behind the house except the black, chain-link fence. Oh—and the moving shadows of two intruders.

Rapper's heart beat rapidly.

When Rapper announced someone was sneaking around outside, Karla's dad flinched. Then he jumped up, screeching his chair across the floor. In one swift movement, he popped open a long, vertical compartment by the back door and retrieved a hefty, silver, laser rifle. Rapper jumped back at the sight of the weapon. It was slightly worn, but shiny. Rapper had seen weapons like this one before. Its power stemmed from light combustion within a mirrored cartridge fixed inside the barrel. It was powerful...powerful enough to make Rapper want to stay a good distance away from anyone firing it.

Mr. Fenwood slapped the door open button. The back door quickly slid aside.

"This is one night those thieves'll never forget!" he shouted, running out the door.

Rapper watched the middle-aged man bound down the wooden stairs, shouting loudly and waving his weapon. The mist turned into a light rain, quickly soaking Mr. Fenwood's shirt.

"Aren't you going to do something?!" Karla shouted at Rapper. He turned around and saw the concerned look on her face.

"What do you want me to do?"

"I thought you were a Superkid!"

"I *am* a Superkid!"

"Then do something!" she shouted.

Karla was right. Rapper should do *something*. Besides, he wanted to find the thieves, and he didn't want Mr. Fenwood to shoot anyone with his mammoth laser rifle.

Rapper darted out the door and bounded down the steps.

"God is my refuge and strength, an ever-present help in trouble," he said, quoting Psalm 46:1. He looked around, but heard nothing. Other than the patter of rain falling around him, the evening was eerily silent. He couldn't hear Mr. Fenwood shouting anymore. He looked back up at the house. Karla's silhouette disappeared from the doorway.

Instantly, the Superkid decided to take to the shadows. He didn't want to be mistaken for one of the intruders and get shot by Mr. Fenwood's bazooka.

Rapper took slow shuffles around the side of the house. He could hear his feet sink lightly into the gravel. Cold rain sank into his brown hair and a trickle crawled down the back of his neck. He shivered.

"I'm a Superkid," Rapper said loud enough for himself to hear. "I will not be afraid or dismayed, for my God is with me wherever I go." Joshua 1:9 always comforted Rapper.

Rapper came around the front of the house. He looked around. The operators' booths looked like hollow boxes. The junk piles still appeared as miniature mountains, now glistening in the moonlight like piles of sweating soda cans.

Another step forward and Rapper froze. Something was under his foot. He bent down. One glance at the item was all it took. Rapper knew what it was. It made him shiver. It made his head swim. It made his heart beat even faster.

It was a knife. A Viper's knife.

Rapper picked it up.

Memories flooded Rapper's mind. Scenes of his time with the Vipers flashed before his eyes. He could almost smell the stench of the large caverns under the city where the Vipers lived. His memory zipped back to the undercity gangs—how they had their own set of rules...rules you *had* to obey, or suffer the consequences. The empty feeling of loneliness gripped his heart, like it had during that time in his life...it was the loneliness all young gang members found...instead of the love they craved. Rapper shook his head. He wanted no part of it anymore.

Commander Kellie and the Superkids told him about God's love and gave him hope. He got out after he made Jesus his Lord. It wasn't easy, but Rapper did it...even though the devil stole his brother first.

Standing in the rain, with the knife in one hand, Rapper reached with his other hand to the back of his neck. He could feel the scar where he had once worn the Vipers' tattoo to prove his loyalty. The tattoo was an olive-green snake, coiled within itself, with an angry "V" for eyebrows and a flickering, red tongue. But that symbol had been removed. Rapper was no longer a Viper. That junk was completely missing from his life—thank God. Now, he was a Superkid. He was a Christian. The devil no longer had a hold on him. God had made him prosperous in his spirit, soul and body. Rapper winced as he focused his thoughts.

The Superkid spun the knife around in his hand. He shoved it into one of the loops on his rain-soaked overalls.

Clink!

Rapper froze. *Where did that sound come from?*

Slowly, he took one step forward, toward the closest mound of trash. Step-by-silent-step, he made his way around the pile.

Crunch. Rapper heard the footstep. Only...*funny*...it wasn't coming from in front of him, but—

Rapper whirled around and came face to face with a Viper. Both Rapper and the Viper jumped back, startled. Then without a moment's notice, the Viper took off. On instinct, Rapper took off after him, leaping over puddles. Rapper knew most Vipers only carried one knife...and Rapper must have had this Viper's only knife or he would have swiped first and asked questions later.

The Viper wore the traditional Viper outfit. He wore dark shorts, black athletic shoes and a lightweight, dark brown jacket with pockets for electronic gear. And, curiously, he wore a black mask. Rapper had never seen a Viper mask himself. His legs were exposed, revealing his dark-brown skin and muscles. He was a large boy, larger than most. But that didn't intimidate Rapper. He had fought with the best.

Zipping around three more junk piles, the Viper almost lost Rapper. The Superkid kept expecting Mr. Fenwood to burst out of nowhere with his weapon and stop the Viper in his tracks. He hoped it wouldn't happen. Despite the Vipers' reputation, they were people, too...and in this case, just kids.

"Stop!" Rapper cried. "I just want to talk to you!"

The Viper continued forward and then let out an ear-piercing whistle. In a moment, another whistle came from nearby. Ten more strides and both Vipers found each other. They headed for the entrance to the complex.

"Stop!" Rapper cried again. They weren't listening.

Ahead, the chained dogs barked furiously.

A scream! The second Viper, dressed like the one Rapper had been chasing, tripped and fell face-first to the ground. Underneath him, gravel and mud spurt out like a stifled firework.

Rapper immediately stopped in his tracks...but not because the Viper fell. Rapper stopped because the scream was...a female scream. In the rain, Rapper blinked. *Since when did Vipers allow girls in the gang?* Adrenaline flowing through him, Rapper pulled the knife out of his belt loop. He approached the fallen Viper.

"Don't move!" he shouted.

The other Viper was standing still now, not sure what to do.

"Your call, your crew!" Rapper shouted, using undercity terminology to demand the Viper's name.

The fallen Viper was also masked. She pushed herself up on one hand and Rapper could see her black eyes staring out at him. She didn't answer. She turned to look at her companion. The mask was pulled up enough in the back that Rapper could see she had no Viper tattoo. He pointed the knife at her neck.

"Where's your mark of loyalty?" Rapper asked her.

"Let me go," she whispered.

Rapper looked at the other Viper. He was obviously shaken.

"Please, let her go," he begged.

Rapper's forehead wrinkled. "You guys...your voices. You're not kids, are you? You're not Vipers?!"

Ka-BOOOOOOOOMMMMMMMMM!!!!!!!!!!!!!!

A flash of white light and a deafening explosion sent Rapper reeling back. Trash blasted from the nearest trash heap and Rapper lost his balance. He crashed to the ground.

Running footsteps approached and Rapper shook his head. The Vipers were gone without a trace.

Mr. Fenwood came running up, his laser rifle slung on his back. "You all right?!" he cried.

"I almost...had them," he told Mr. Fenwood.

Karla's dad shook his head, helping Rapper up.

"What was that?" Rapper asked.

"Get in quick!" Karla yelled from the front doorway of her house.

Mr. Fenwood waved. Then he turned to Rapper and held his fingers up in the Superkid's face. His forefinger and thumb were barely an inch apart. "You're one lucky kid!" he exclaimed. "You were that close to being hit by lightning!"

Rapper looked up at the deep, dark clouds throwing down rain. Rapper let out a nervous laugh. He almost rapped, but couldn't get it out. Instead, he just said, "Luck had nothing to do with it. The One Who is in me is greater than the one who is in the world," quoting 1 John 4:4.

To Rapper's surprise, Mr. Fenwood clenched his teeth, scowled and stormed away.

"They're gone!" Mr. Fenwood hollered to Karla as he pushed through the rain, heading back to the house.

"That's it?!" Rapper challenged, on his heels. "The Vipers could still be around here somewhere!"

"You can stay out here and get hit by lightning if you want, but I'm not taking a chance." Mr. Fenwood's voice had an edge Rapper hadn't heard before.

Rapper couldn't believe it. "What are the chances of that happening again?"

"It happens 'round here all the time." He threw his hands in the air. "Look around you. There are stacks of metal everywhere." He sounded more frustrated than informative.

Rapper threw his own hands up in frustration. "Father," he prayed aloud, "according to 1 Corinthians 4:5, I pray You would bring to light what is hidden in darkness—and expose the motives of men's hearts."

Mr. Fenwood spun around, jarring Rapper in his tracks. Rain dripped from the ends of his graying hair and his nose.

"Do *not* bring God or any of your 'hocus-pocus' into this," he ordered. His finger pointed sharply in Rapper's face. "I don't need any trouble here. Things are just fine."

Rapper wanted to ask, *You like being robbed?* but words failed him. The sudden, unexpected intensity of Mr. Fenwood left him speechless. *What's eating at this guy?* Rapper wondered.

Karla's dad stared at Rapper angrily. His teeth were clenched behind his lips, defining his jaw line. Rapper stared into his brown eyes, refusing to back down. No one was going to tell him he couldn't pray.

"The Holy Spirit *will* bring things to light," Rapper said sternly, though not much louder than the dripping of the rain.

At once, Karla's father demanded, "Who *are* you?"

Then, like a beam of sunlight through the clouds, the Holy Spirit dropped a revelation into Rapper's heart that nearly brought him to his knees.

"Y-you're...Kentren Fenwood III."

Mr. Fenwood shook his head. "So? I told you that!"

"I knew I had heard your name before...the Holy Spirit just reminded me...you're a legend."

Mr. Fenwood turned around and resumed his walk toward the house. "Sorry, you have me mixed up with someone else."

Rapper matched his pace. "No, I'm sure of it. I recognize the name. Mr. Fenwood, I used to be a member of the Vipers."

"Good, maybe you can tell them to stop robbing my junkyard."

"Mr. Fenwood." Rapper stopped walking. "Mr. Fenwood!"

At Rapper's shout Karla's dad stopped in his tracks. In defiance, he refused to turn around.

"I know who you are. The older Vipers used to talk about you. You're the only man who was bold enough to enter the underground and tell the gangs that money was a lousy god. You told them God wanted them to do well in life, but they had to turn to Jesus. I've heard about you! They say that, like, 12 years ago you turned countless gang members to Christ." Rapper paused. "The leaders hated it, but you did it anyway. You weren't afraid. Then...one day...you just stopped coming to minister. That's you, isn't it?"

Mr. Fenwood stayed quiet, not moving a muscle.

"But why did you stop coming?" Rapper persisted. "If you continued ministering, I might have found Jesus by your ministry...and others might have...like my brother... They *needed* you. Why did you stop ministering?"

"That's not me anymore," he said quietly. "What I did may not be right, but it had to happen. Not everyone's a hero. I had my reasons for what I did...things I couldn't give up."

"Things?" Rapper repeated. "You gave up ministering for *things?* Look, Matthew 6:33 says if you seek first God's kingdom and His righteousness, He'll give you—"

"I don't want to hear it!" Mr. Fenwood spat, spinning back around to face the Superkid.

Rapper felt like he'd been socked in the stomach. "I—I don't understand," he admitted. "You were a great man of faith...now you're not even serving the Lord... How could you just let go of your relationship with Jesus?" Suddenly his own voice took on an edge. Rapper was careful to walk in love, but sometimes love had to be tough...and confrontational. "Proverbs 4:23 says that above *all else,* you must guard your heart. You can't let—" Rapper stopped himself. He didn't want to sound overbearing. "I'm just saying, giving up left those kids thinking that's the way Christians treat people and—"

"I'm not responsible for those kids!" Mr. Fenwood shouted.

Rapper wiped the rain off his face. "Who are you responsible for?!" he retorted. Maybe overbearing wasn't so bad once in a while. "How about Karla?! How about sharing Jesus with her? How about raising her in the Word? You can let yourself go without Jesus, but how can you give up on her?"

Mr. Fenwood swung an arm in the direction of the house. "I have *not* given up on Karla! I *love* Karla! No one's going to tell me how to raise my daughter!" Fenwood pointed his finger in Rapper's face again. "You don't know anything about me!"

"I know you used to be a minister of the gospel and you gave it up for *things!* I know you lost your temper when you heard me pray! That reveals worlds of information to me!"

"Who do you think you *are?!* You're just a *kid!*"

"It's in the *Bible,*" Rapper said, "and I know that because the Word lives in me. I'm a *Superkid.*"

Mr. Fenwood threw his head back and groaned. He waved his hands in the air. "A *Superkid?!?!* Perfect!" Mr. Fenwood looked down at Rapper. "Get off my property," he said, suddenly hard.

"What?" Rapper inquired.

"Get off my property!" he shouted.

"No!" Karla cried. She was outside now, too. The rain was slowly soaking her. Her thin lips were drawn down. "He's my friend!"

"Karla!" Mr. Fenwood shouted in surprise. "H-how long have you been there?"

"Long enough to know you don't want my friend here."

"Is he *really* your friend from school?" Mr. Fenwood challenged his daughter. "Or is that a lie? Last I knew, Superkids attend their own private school—Superkid Academy."

"Look," Rapper broke in, "I don't want you two to fight. I can leave. No big deal."

Karla kicked the gravel and began to cry. She turned around shouting, "He's my friend!" and ran up the crooked, wooden-planked steps, into the house.

"Karla!" Mr. Fenwood pleaded. "Karla!" She didn't answer. Rapper saw the light to her room flash on, shining out from the side of the house. Mr. Fenwood turned to face Rapper. Rapper shook his head.

"One night," Mr. Fenwood said coolly. "You can stay tonight and then leave tomorrow." With that, he said nothing more. He headed up the wooden planks toward the front door. Rapper reluctantly followed.

Things, Rapper pondered.

Atop the antique daybed, Rapper lay on an itchy wool blanket. He couldn't sleep. It wasn't the storm that kept him awake—in fact, it didn't thunder or lightning the rest of the night. It was Rapper's own heart that kept him from rest. As Rapper's wide eyes panned the simple room, he took in all the shadows and angles created by the furniture, the sparse decor and the small window opposite the dresser.

When daylight finally came, the shadows would disappear...or, at least, be moved to create a different angle. Rapper wondered if this is what happened to the shadows in a person's heart. Were they always there, just moved to different angles when the sun shone in?

Rapper shook his head. No. He knew better. Second Corinthians 5:17 said that when the Life and Light of Jesus touch your heart, He takes the shadows—the junk of the old life—away. He replaces the old life with His own, new life. Rapper felt he knew that better than anyone. He had fallen a great distance from the Lord...but when He made Jesus his Lord, he was instantly rescued. The shadows were wiped completely away.

But, Rapper wondered, *isn't that what happened to Mr. Fenwood, too? Hadn't he known the power of God in his life? Then why would he throw it away for* **things?** Rapper was sure he could never do that. Never. But then...he never would expect a powerful minister like Mr. Fenwood to do it, either. *What had happened? Why had Mr. Fenwood allowed the junk back into his life? Why would someone willingly do that?* Rapper shook his head, pondering the mystery.

He sat up. He felt restless. He felt uneasy.

Throwing his legs over the side of the bed, Rapper yawned. *I should have just had Commander Kellie pick me up,* he thought. But he didn't know all this would happen. Besides, he was still very interested in figuring out what was going on around the strange junkyard.

Rapper touched a small, metal lamp on the table beside the bed and it flickered on, casting light across the room. Shadows moved to new positions. *Maybe,* Rapper pondered, *Mr. Fenwood never really knew Jesus in the first place.* Rapper stood, dismissing the thought. He knew he couldn't truly be the judge of that.

The Superkid felt aches beginning to form in his legs. He walked toward the mirror and stared at himself. His brown eyes were bloodshot, and his normally spiked, brown hair was going every which way since hitting the pillow. He was wearing an old T-shirt and shorts Karla had left him on his bed. He hadn't seen her since the "blowup." Rapper took a deep breath. It had been a long time since he had felt that furious. Somehow, Mr. Fenwood had struck something within him that caused him to react that way.

Quite frankly, the whole thing made Rapper uncomfortable. If Kentren Fenwood III, minister of the gospel, could lose his faith...couldn't Rapper, too? Rapper checked his heart. He always weighed the consequences of the *things* of life. If something new came up, before he was willing to go along with it, he always asked himself, *Can I afford this spiritually?* If he thought the *thing* would steal his time from the Word and prayer, the answer was "no."

But what if things got tough again like they had when his parents divorced? Would he resort to his old ways? Would he trade his faith for food? Money? Love? What if he didn't live at Superkid Academy? School kids bend to peer pressure all the time. Could he, too? Could he? If things got really tough?

Rapper's fingertips tapped the dresser. He picked up his Superkid wings. He looked forward to wearing them again—to getting back in his uniform and back to "normal life." Rapper's other hand moved to the Viper knife he'd found outside. He looked at the Superkid wings in one hand, the Viper knife in the other. Here were the two parts of his life—the new and the old. Rapper closed his fist around the Superkid wings.

"I don't want to lose this," he said to himself. "Others may forget what they have, but I don't want to. Holy Spirit, show me how to always keep You first."

The silence of the room rang in Rapper's ears. Then, ever so gently, the Holy Spirit reminded Rapper of 2 Timothy 2:3.

Endure hardness like a good soldier, He whispered.

Rapper nodded. "I will."

I'm looking throughout the whole earth to show Myself strong on behalf of those whose hearts are loyal to Me, He added, mentioning 2 Chronicles 16:9.

For a brief moment, Rapper closed his eyes. "My heart will stay loyal," he promised. "I want Your strength to show through me."

Rapper looked around the room for a Bible, but didn't see one. He wasn't surprised. Still, the Word was in his heart. He remembered Mark 4:14-19. It talked about making sure the ground of your heart was always ready to receive. He had to keep it clean from all the rocks, all the weeds, all the junk that would try to spring up and stop the Word from working in him. Rapper wanted his heart to always be fertile ground. He wondered if Mr. Fenwood had ever hoped that hope. Had Mr. Fenwood ever looked in the mirror like Rapper and longed to serve the Lord wholeheartedly? Had he ever had any inkling that one day he would stop serving Him?

Rapper jumped as he heard the thump. He looked at the clock on the end table. It was nearly 2 a.m. *What was that?* The sound came from next door...in Karla's room. Rapper grabbed the Viper knife and took a step toward the door. Then he stopped. He looked at the knife again and placed it back on the dresser. Then he headed out the door.

The hallway was dark. Rapper peered in the direction of Mr. Fenwood's room. The door was closed. Rapper looked at Karla's door. It was closed, too. But Rapper knew he'd heard something. He decided it was better to be safe than sorry. He knocked on Karla's door.

A long pause was followed by another thump, shuffling sounds and then, again, another thump.

"Karla?" Rapper whispered as loud as he could without waking her father.

Suddenly the door shifted aside, flooding the hallway with light from within the room. Karla was there, looking disheveled. She was wearing a T-shirt and shorts, too.

"What's wrong?" she asked. "It's 2 a.m."

Rapper's eyes drifted into her room. "I know it," he said matter-of-factly. "So what are you doing up?"

Karla shifted a little to the side, looking uncomfortable. Rapper looked over her shoulder. Something mysterious was happening and Rapper wanted to get to the bottom of it.

"I just had trouble sleeping," Karla explained.

"I remember your dad saying that happens a lot," Rapper pushed.

Karla added, "Well, our fight tonight didn't help any."

Rapper looked around the room. It was simple, like Rapper's room, but colorful. Karla's bed was across from the door, next to a large, sliding window. A desk was on the far side of it, with several papers on top, a few books and a few drawings.

"Hey," Rapper said, "thanks for sticking up for me earlier. But you know, I don't want you disobeying your dad for my sake. Ephesians 6:1 says to obey your parents—then things will go well for you and you'll live a long, full life on earth. As long as your dad's not asking you to do anything against what the Bible says, obedience is important." Rapper added that last point to see if it spurred anything in Karla.

"I'll be out of here one day anyway," she muttered.

In the background, Rapper spotted some books on Karla's desk. "You have a Bible?" he asked.

She shook her head.

He folded his arms as a shiver crept up his back. "Your room has a draft."

Karla shrugged.

Rapper spotted a picture on Karla's desk. From the distance, it looked like it was in crayon—a standard-looking, square house with a chimney and birds flying outside, by a tree. Down the house's door, from top to bottom, she had drawn thick, black lines. In the drawing, it looked like the window was open.

"What's that?" Rapper asked, pointing toward it. "You an artist, Karla?"

Karla shifted, blocking Rapper's view as she muttered something like "just a stupid drawing."

Rapper could tell she wasn't going to give him any clues. Still chilled, he looked over to see if the real window to her room was open. It wasn't.

"Hey, there's a Bible!" Rapper said, pointing toward a small, tattered, blue Bible laying on the floor by the window. He wanted to go in and grab it, but the gentleman in him wouldn't permit it.

Karla's brown eyes grew wide and she raced over to the Bible. She picked it up and put it behind her back.

"Wha—"

"Don't tell him, please don't tell him," Karla begged.

Rapper blinked, not moving from the doorway. "What's going on?"

Karla turned, shaking her head. She put the Bible on her desk. "Promise you won't tell."

"Karla, having a Bible isn't a crime."

"Shhh! It's a risk," she responded.

"What aren't you telling me?" Rapper inquired.

She shook her head again. "Please go."

Rapper bit his lip and started to turn. Then he stopped, turned back around and stated, "I want to help if I can, Karla. I don't know what's going on here, but I'm going to figure it out."

Karla looked at the floor, thought for a moment, then walked over and hit the door close button.

"Just be careful," she whispered. The door slid shut, leaving Rapper in the dark.

After his one-sided talk with Karla, Rapper returned to his room and fell asleep, exhausted. The next morning, he was awakened by the sun pouring through the tiny window in his room, reflecting off the mirror and hitting him in the eyes. It felt good to have a new day before him.

Upon opening the door to his room, he found a red sweat suit, folded in a square, lying in the doorway. He grabbed it, wondering where his Superkid uniform was, and showered. Rapper's body didn't ache like he thought it would had he not prayed, and he was thankful that God's Word was always true. He quickly dried off and slipped into the sweat suit. When he pulled the sweat shirt over his head, he gasped—the front of the shirt was peppered with little, embroidered, striped candy canes...with green bows.

"If only my friends could see me now," he moaned. He pulled on his Academy-issued socks and wondered if his shoes, out on the back porch, were dry yet.

When Rapper emerged from the bathroom, he heard silverware clanking in the kitchen. He strolled out, feeling fresh. Karla and her dad were seated catty-corner to each other at the oblong, metal, kitchen table.

They were both fresh for the day, too. Karla wore jeans again, this time with a purple-flowered, white shirt. Her father wore overalls again, with a gray shirt. They were both munching on toast and a medium-sized bowl of oatmeal was at each setting. One setting—opposite Mr. Fenwood—was open, with an empty bowl and plate. Rapper took this to be his own. He approached the table and smiled. Mr. Fenwood looked up and down at Rapper's outfit and grimaced. He made some kind of judgmental groan. Rapper kept his smile on. Karla smiled weakly at Rapper, but didn't say anything.

Rapper took inventory of the kitchen. A pan of oatmeal was on the stove and a photonic toaster stood beside it. It had been a while since he had eaten honest-to-goodness-cook-it-yourself oatmeal. He walked over and slopped a couple heaping spoonfuls of the hot, thick, lumpy meal into his bowl. He dropped two slices of toast into the photonic toaster and programmed the intensity of toasting. Within 15 seconds it was completed. He marched his food to the table and sat down. As an afterthought, he got up and fetched himself a glass of water.

No one had yet said anything, leaving a tone of edginess in the small room. Rapper buttered his toast. He looked at Karla and her dad. Neither looked up from their meal. Rapper bowed his head and said a silent thanks for the breakfast.

"Nice morning," Rapper said cheerfully after his prayer. Both Mr. Fenwood and Karla stopped chewing and looked straight at Rapper. He stopped chewing and smiled. They both went back to their meals. The next five minutes of the breakfast consisted of chewing, swallowing and the clinking of silverware...nothing more.

Then, Mr. Fenwood put down his silverware and wiped his mouth on a paper napkin. He leaned back in his chair and glared at Rapper. Rapper stopped chewing and smiled again.

"Well," Karla's dad said, "I guess since you're a Superkid, you won't be riding to school with Karla."

Karla protested his question by putting her spoon on the table with a slap.

"Actually," Rapper said, glancing from Karla to her dad, "I'll just ride into town on the hoverbus with Karla and call for a ride from there."

Karla winced.

"What?" her dad asked.

Karla turned to Rapper with a sheepish look on her face. "I just remembered this morning that I didn't wash your outfit."

"You're doing his wash?" Mr. Fenwood complained.

"He got dirty in *our* junkyard," Karla returned.

Mr. Fenwood wadded his napkin into a ball. "It's not a junkyard. It's a disassembly plant."

Karla's head tilted toward her dad in disbelief.

"No problem," Rapper said. "I can just carry my wet clothes with me and return this to you later." He pointed to the candy cane-studded, red sweat suit he wore.

"He's wearing your clothes?" Karla's dad questioned, irritable.

"Just old clothes," Karla said.

"He's not leaving with your clothes."

Karla ignored her dad and looked at Rapper. "I put your clothes in the washer about 15 minutes ago. They should be done in a while. But I think you'll miss the hoverbus."

Rapper looked at Mr. Fenwood. "I'll just call and get a ride into town when they're ready," he said, solving the problem.

Mr. Fenwood smiled mockingly. "Wonderful. We get to be graced with your presence for a little longer."

Rapper bit his tongue. Mr. Fenwood got up, tossed his dishes in the sink and walked out the back door.

Karla huffed.

"What did I do?" Rapper asked.

Karla shook her head. "It's not what you did," she said softly. "It's what *he* did."

The front door slid open, interrupting any further inquiry from Rapper. It was big Buddy, back in overalls, angling his thumb over his shoulder. "Hoverbus is here, Karla!" he shouted. "Zeke and I saw 'em comin' on the way in." Rapper could hear the junkyard dogs barking in the background.

Karla smiled at Rapper and grabbed her book bag.

"I'm sorry things didn't work out," she said, dis-appointed. "One day they will. I really believe that. Thanks anyway. Bye, Rapper." Karla darted out the front door, shouting another goodbye to the Superkid on the way out.

Rapper suddenly found himself alone in the kitchen. *What is going on in this household?* he wondered again. He looked at the table, still full of dirty dishes. "Don't worry, guys," he said aloud to no one in particular. "I'll clean up." And with that, Rapper did the dishes.

▲ ▲ ▲

On his way out to get a breath of fresh air, Rapper checked his uniform, only to find out the machine hadn't finished its cycle. Soap and water dripped off the outfit. He tossed it back in the washer and let it continue its cycle. He found his shoes and they were still a little damp. Rapper put them on anyway.

With plenty of time on his hands and a full junkyard before him, Rapper decided to ask Buddy and Zeke, Mr. Fenwood's workers, some questions. Rapper knew it wasn't his job to solve the mystery of the missing junk, but his curiosity begged him for answers. And for whatever reason, Mr. Fenwood had something against God and Superkid Academy—maybe a conviction would give him reason to reconsider. Maybe.

The Superkid headed directly for Buddy's booth—a small, square shack that had the ability to raise up on stilts so Buddy could see over the entire junkyard. Along the way, Rapper passed two large piles of junk as his feet pressed the moist ground. The sun was rising hot in the east, but the air was still cool on his cheeks. In the damp shoes, his feet felt cold.

When Rapper reached Buddy, the junkyard operator was already 20 feet up in the air, sitting comfortably. Rapper yelled his name and the wide-faced man peered over. He held out a finger, motioning to Rapper to wait a second. With the flip of a couple controls, Buddy guided the flying, remote-controlled, magnetic disc to a holding place. He pulled a lever and slowly his booth lowered. Farther down the row, Zeke looked on with interest. By the time Buddy was level with the ground, though, Zeke had gone back to work.

"Stickin' around, eh?" Buddy asked.

Rapper nodded. "For a little longer anyway."

Above his thick, black mustache, Buddy's nose crinkled and his eyes narrowed as he took in Rapper's apparel.

Rapper folded his arms, trying to cover up a few of the striped candy canes. "It's on loan," he explained. Buddy nodded as if he understood.

"Uh, I just wanted to ask you a few questions," Rapper continued. Buddy looked at him blankly.

"So," Rapper began, "I was just wondering how long you've worked here."

"I don't think there's any jobs available," Buddy countered. "Just me and Zeke are the only ones Mr. Fenwood needs 'round."

"Oh, I'm not looking for employment," Rapper explained. "I was just wondering."

Buddy chewed on his bottom lip, measuring Rapper's inquiry. He shrugged. "I been here 10 years as of March. Me and Zeke, we were the first ones Fenwood hired."

Karla's words were triggered in Rapper's memory. "Actually, Karla said Mr. Fenwood has been here for 12 years—ever since she was born."

Another shrug. "Nope. Been 'bout 10 years. When he hired us, Karla was already a kid—walkin', I mean."

"You ever know Mrs. Fenwood?" Rapper asked.

"I don't ask questions like you do," Buddy stated. "I just work 'cuz Fenwood gives me a job. I never seen a Missus. I dunno. Maybe she divorced him or maybe Karla's adopted. Shoot, maybe the Missus died or somethin'. Shame if she did. Fenwood's a good man."

Rapper nodded. This was going nowhere fast. "You say he's a good man...you ever know him when he was a preacher?"

That got a chuckle that shook Buddy's belly. "I've never known Fenwood to be the praying sort. Maybe you got him mixed up with someone else."

"I'll let you get back to work," Rapper promised. "But one more thing—you have any clue who the robbers are?"

Buddy hit a lever, causing his booth to start lifting. He shook his head. "All it takes is finding the glass slipper."

"The what?"

"The glass slipper—that fits the foot," Buddy said as he rose. "I've seen the robbers' footprints around the yard. Here and there. To find the robbers, all you have to do is find whose feet fit the prints."

As Buddy continued upward, Rapper stood, momentarily stunned. He hadn't even thought to look for footprints! Rapper looked up at Buddy. He hadn't thought to check out the size of his feet. Of course, if it were Buddy, he would make sure the footprints matched someone else before he gave away a clue like that. Rapper let out a sigh.

Suppose for a minute it was Buddy, he thought. *He had access to the front gate. He knew the layout of the property. He probably even knew which junked cars contained autocomms. He'd know how to get past security cameras and alarms and more. And what better way to frame someone than to place false footprints around the yard and then point a young sleuth to them?*

But what would be Buddy's motivation? Money? Rapper doubted it. Buddy didn't even wear a ring... which is also why Rapper figured he wasn't married. And whoever was dressing up as Vipers clearly had a female accomplice. Not to mention the fact that Buddy was quite a large man—not at all like one of the Vipers he'd chased earlier. Rapper shook his head. It didn't make sense for it to be Buddy.

Rapper looked over at Zeke's booth. It was a little larger than Buddy's because it had more controls inside. Best he could tell, Zeke was primarily in charge of the conveyor belt. Maybe he had seen something suspicious. Rapper headed toward him.

Zeke watched Rapper approach, never taking his eyes off the Superkid. Rapper already felt ridiculous in the candy cane and bow-covered duds, but Zeke made him feel obvious, too.

Rapper waved upon approach and leaned in an open window. "You have a few seconds?" Rapper asked. Zeke didn't answer, but shut down the noisy conveyor belt. Rapper peeked in the booth and checked out the size of Zeke's feet. They were medium-sized and wide. He wore boots.

Zeke yawned. With one hand he scratched the twiggy hair on his white scalp. With the other, he scratched his armpit.

"Yeah?" he drawled out.

Rapper pulled back a bit. "Zeke?"

"Yeah?"

"I was wondering if I could ask you a few questions?"

"K."

"Buddy tells me you've been working here since the beginning?"

"Yeah."

"Was that 10 or 12 years ago?"

Zeke counted on his fingers. When he got to the tenth, he stopped. He looked at his feet. "'Bout 10," he said, drawling each word. He looked like an ape, but he talked like a snail...slowly!

He said 10 years, too, Rapper thought. *So why did Karla lead Rapper to believe she was born here?* But then Rapper wondered if that was even significant...or was he just being picky?

"You ever know Karla's mom?" Rapper asked. He knew it wouldn't lead him to the answer about the robbers, but he was curious—it was another point in which Karla had been very evasive.

"Nope." Zeke punctuated the "P."

Rapper tapped the window ledge. "I don't suppose you knew Mr. Fenwood when he was a preacher, did you?"

Zeke sniffed, but showed no signs of surprise at the revelation. "Nope."

"Well, what about the robberies?" Rapper asked him. He had already concluded that Zeke had no part in them. When Rapper had chased the "Vipers," he saw the back of their necks—both were dark-skinned. But Zeke's skin was as white as the surface of an egg. "You know anything about the robberies?" Rapper pushed.

Suddenly Zeke's eyes lit up. His arms lifted as he began making motions with his hands.

"I've seen 'em," he whispered.

Rapper's mouth almost dropped. "You what?! You've seen them? You mean you know what the robbers look like?"

Zeke nodded. His eyes shot side to side as he said, "They're about this tall." He lifted his hands to his chest. "And they got big feet and black eyes."

"When did you see them?" Rapper asked.

"Late at night," his voice dropped back to a whisper. "They always come late at night."

"And do what?"

"Take parts for experiments."

"Experiments?"

"Experiments," he confirmed.

"They need autocomms for experiments?"

Zeke nodded. "But they get in here, quiet as a mouse 'cuz they come over the fence."

"You mean over the laser beams?"

"Way over," he said, motioning a flying motion with his hands. "That's how they get past the dogs." His eyes shifted to the right, then to the left. "And they're watching us now."

Rapper looked around. Buddy was working in the booth behind them, but there was no other sign of intrusion. "What? Can you tell me more about how they look? Big feet and black eyes isn't much to go on."

"I can tell you this: You never want to meet them."

"Why not?"

"'Cuz they got lasers that come out of their eyes."

"Huh?"

"And their skin is scaly and green and they come from a planet near the star Cirrus! They want to take over earth and use our water for fuel! In fact...oh, no! Here comes their ship now!" Zeke pointed a shaky hand and then dove into his booth. Rapper whirled around to see Buddy's remote-controlled, silver disc rounding the corner.

Then, like a pirate, Zeke let out a barrage of laughter as he held his stomach and pointed at Rapper. "Har! Har! Har! Har! Har! Har!"

Rapper twisted his mouth and waved goodbye. So much for a serious talk with Zeke. Still, Rapper did gain something. Zeke said that the robbers got past the dogs by going over the fence. That may or may not be true, but the robbers *did* somehow get past the dogs. Because those dogs barked when *anyone* got near. But how? Rapper fully intended to find out. He walked toward the rear of the Fenwood household to find the area where he first saw the robbers. Maybe he'd find one of their footprints etched in the soft soil. And maybe he could follow it. And maybe he'd start finding some answers.

The back of the Fenwood's bi-level dwelling was mostly siding, with cutouts for the back door and a few windows. Rapper recognized his window as the tiny cutout near the left edge. The window by the kitchen door was in front of Rapper, at the right of the building. Rapper passed the window to Mr. Fenwood's room, farther around the side. He deduced Karla's window was around the other side. Rapper looked at the kitchen door. From there was where he'd first seen the so-called "Vipers."

He looked around the ground for any sign of footprints. And he found them. Many of them. Everywhere. There were at least five shapes and sizes. Rapper huffed. Even his own footprints were there. Rapper kept his eyes open for anything unusual. Anything out of the ordinary that could help him.

And he found it.

Along the very back of the house, behind the garage area, Rapper saw two sets of footprints, one on top of the other. Apparently one of the Vipers led and the other followed. Then, as Rapper followed the same footprints out into the open, they became muddled with everyone else's footprints. They were moving from the house to...somewhere...and on their way there, they passed the back door where Rapper had seen them. Rapper looked around. The only structure they could have been heading to was a midsized warehouse about 100 feet away. Rapper wondered what was inside it.

Rapper turned around and looked the other way. Another thought occurred to him. Maybe the footprint trail would show him where they'd entered the junkyard. Rapper decided the best idea would be to retrace the crooks' steps from the beginning. Carefully, he followed the footprints backward. They led around the side of the house past a pile of junk near Karla's window and on into the main grounds of the junkyard. Two or three times, he thought he'd lost the trail, but then he would see another footprint nearby. "Thank You, Jesus," he whispered every time he saw another footprint.

Best Rapper could tell, the footprints stopped by four or five junk piles along the way, probably to search broken-down hovercars for autocomms.

He followed the footprints farther and was surprised to discover they came directly through the front gate. When the junkyard dogs saw Rapper, they began to snarl and bark. Rapper thanked God they were chained up while Karla was at school. He didn't bother approaching them. But then Rapper's head twisted as he noticed something highly unusual: The junkyard alarm box was mounted inside the fence, on the same post where the dogs were chained.

On the other side of the fence, Rapper saw the robbers' footprints. They led right up to the alarm box. Dog footprints were everywhere on the inside. It appeared the robbers were walking up to the dogs, reaching through the fence, disabling the alarm and then walking straight through—without the dogs barking even once.

Rapper scratched his head. "Father God, according to Proverbs 2:6, give me wisdom, I pray. In Jesus' Name." Rapper quietly listened to hear if the Holy Spirit revealed anything to him. The Superkid knew he couldn't solve the mystery without His help. Without Him, Rapper could do nothing. Briefly, Rapper wondered if Mr. Fenwood ever used to talk to the Lord like this. Rapper shook his head and focused his thoughts on his investigation.

OK, so it had to be someone the dogs knew. But when Rapper got out the food for the dogs the night before, Karla said the dogs even barked at her dad. So it had to be someone the dogs knew *and* liked. It just didn't make sense. Someone had obviously stolen the code and found a way to pacify the dogs.

Rapper thought it was time to let Mr. Fenwood know his security was being penetrated.

Rapper headed back into the junkyard, making his way between the mountains of trash. About halfway to Buddy's booth, the dogs finally stopped barking at him. Rapper thought about going to Zeke's booth instead, but he wasn't sure if Zeke would give him a real answer. When he arrived, it took Buddy a few minutes before he saw him. Eventually, he rode the booth down and smiled again at Rapper. "Hey kid, thought you left again."

Rapper looked down at his outfit. He had almost forgotten about his clothes. "I'm about ready to leave," he said truthfully. He knew once he told Mr. Fenwood about the security breach, the man would probably tell him he shouldn't be messing around his junkyard anymore. He would be grateful, Rapper imagined, but he wouldn't let Rapper know it. Besides, he could take it from there.

Rapper asked, "Have you seen Mr. Fenwood around anywhere?"

Buddy angled his thumb over his shoulder. "He's probably in his office. It's in the warehouse behind us here."

"Great," Rapper replied. "I was heading over there anyway."

▲   ▲   ▲

The warehouse was a medium-sized, sheet-metal structure with an angled roof, higher on the left than the right. It wasn't fancy, but it kept its contents dry—the perfect storage answer for a junkyard business. As Rapper approached, he stopped midstep as he discovered another set of the robbers' tracks. At once, the Superkid wondered how old the tracks were. Were they from the night before? Could they be even more recent than that? What if they'd come back to "pay" Mr. Fenwood for the scare he'd given them last night? Rapper picked up his pace.

When Rapper reached the slab of concrete in front of the warehouse, he grabbed the rickety, old-style door and swung it open.

"Mr. Fenwood?" he called out. There was no answer. But there appeared to be no trouble. There was nothing obviously messed up, no mud on the cement ground. Rapper let out a long breath. Well, that was good news anyway. He called out Mr. Fenwood's name again just to be sure. The only response was Rapper's own echo.

The majority of the warehouse was filled with boxes, stacked one atop another. As far back as Rapper could see, the cardboard towers created a metropolis. Pale, fluorescent lights hung in strips between the rows of boxes.

To Rapper's right, however, a 12x12-foot nook was cut out of the boxes. A wide and deep metal desk sat directly in the center. Behind it was a metal cabinet with a lock. A lamp, ComPhone, monthly calendar and other papers were on the desk. A short filing cabinet at the side had a coffee maker on top. Rapper guessed this was Mr. Fenwood's "seat of command"—his work desk for performing the various paper transactions needed with his business.

Rapper walked over to the desk. His eye was instantly drawn to the small photo frame at the front. It faced inward, so Rapper walked behind the desk to look at it. He figured it best to not touch anything that belonged to

Karla's dad...especially with the way he felt about Rapper right now. Rapper bent down and looked straight across at the picture.

It was the picture of a young Karla—Rapper guessed she couldn't have been more than 2 or 3 years old. Toddler Karla was smiling wide at the camera. She wore plaits, her black hair sticking out of her head like pompoms on sticks. A waxy, red heart, drawn in crayon, surrounded Karla's head. It was crooked and lopsided—most likely drawn by Karla herself. Rapper smiled. It was the only photo he had seen around the Fenwood household. Again the question nagged at Rapper: Why would this minister give up his relationship with the Lord for *things?*

In Jeremiah 2:13, God said, "My people have committed two sins: They have forsaken me, the spring of living water, and have dug their own cisterns, broken cisterns that cannot hold water." Before now, Rapper never really understood that verse. But somehow, in this mess with the Fenwoods, it suddenly made sense. God told Jeremiah His people had sinned twice: First, they stopped spending time with Him. Then they tried to live on their own. They got so busy with things, they didn't spend time with Him. Rapper knew it could happen. It happened then. It happened now. But could it happen to *him? A Superkid?*

Rapper's gaze dropped across the ComPhone to the calendar. He noticed yesterday's date was circled. It was the day Rapper arrived. Rapper didn't know what it meant. Then, on the 30th of the month, a small, blue "P" was drawn by the date. Other notes on the calendar were what one would expect from a business: scrawled notes about utilities due, pick-ups and deliveries. The guy really needed a computer.

When Rapper straightened up, the back of his leg hit the chair. He moved around it, then pushed it back to the desk. The chair's rollers went faster than he expected and the chair hit the desk with a slam. Karla's picture fell onto its back. *Clink!* Something dropped on the floor. Rapper set the picture upright again. Then, he reached to the floor to recover the fallen item.

The fluorescent light above Rapper glared off the shiny object: a tiny silver key. Rapper picked it up. Where had it come from? Rapper looked around the desk. He knew it wasn't just sitting on top—he would have seen it.

Rapper's heart skipped a beat. He heard someone approaching. Rapper's head rushed—where to put the key? If Mr. Fenwood caught him standing behind his desk, holding his key, that would be all he needed— Rapper would be in for it. It would just be adding fuel to Mr. Fenwood's fire. Without time to think of a better plan, Rapper resorted to what he'd seen someone do once on a comedy show. He shoved the chair aside, dove under the desk and replaced the chair.

The flimsy, old-style door crashed open and Rapper heard hefty footsteps walk into the room. The footsteps, to Rapper's dismay, came around the desk. The chair rolled aside and the person dropped into it. Rapper's heart was beating fast and he could feel a cold sweat coming on. Rapper saw the occupant's hands and immediately recognized them as belonging to Mr. Fenwood. The man slid forward in the chair, his legs sliding under the wide desk. Rapper pressed his body against the metal furniture. He considered showing himself and playing it off as a joke. But Rapper didn't think Karla's dad would think it was funny. What's a Superkid doing hiding in his office, under his desk, with his key?!

A few long minutes passed when suddenly Rapper saw Mr. Fenwood's hand appear. His fingers danced along the underside of his chair, searching for something. The key! Rapper saw a tiny notch in the chair—just big enough to hide a key in. It must have dropped out when Rapper jarred the chair.

Carefully, Rapper leaned forward, trying not to touch the man's pant leg. He pressed the key on the underside of the chair, into the notch. He retrieved his fingers just in time to miss Mr. Fenwood's hand going after the key once more. A second later the key was retrieved and Mr. Fenwood swiveled around in his chair and stood up.

Rapper heard the key insert in the lock and pop it open. The tall cabinet creaked open and Mr. Fenwood

began to mumble. "...two...ree...four...sev...eight, nine."
The cabinet closed again and he re-clamped the lock. He
dropped into the chair again and rolled back into
position facing the desk. Rapper scrunched back as far
as he could, holding his breath.

Rapper heard the tones of a number being dialed on
the ComPhone.

There was a click and then someone answered.

The voice said, "This is Han—"

"We had nine more stolen this month," Mr. Fenwood
interrupted in a sorrowful voice.

"You've got to get better security," the voice
responded.

"We've got what we can afford."

"You need better or we'll have to drop you, Kentren."

Mr. Fenwood sounded suddenly irritated. "I have a
right to that money—my policy says so."

"Whoa-whoa. I know what your policy says. You'll
get your money by the 30th as usual. But let me tell you,
this has gone on way too long. You're turning heads."

"Turn 'em back."

"I can't, Kentren."

The ComPhone clicked off. Mr. Fenwood slammed
his fist on the metal desk, causing the small space Rapper
occupied to thunder. Rapper tensed up.

The hand appeared under the chair again, found the
notch and shoved the key into place. The chair rolled

back quickly, screeching. Mr. Fenwood got up and left the room. Rapper waited until the door settled its banging.

Slowly, Rapper pushed the chair aside and crawled out from under the desk. He looked around and waited until his heart rate returned to normal. He looked at the ComPhone. He put his finger over the tiny camera and hit redial.

A man's face appeared on the screen. He had a black beard, trimmed close, and a balding head. "This is Hank and you've reached Insurecom Insurance! How may I help you? Hey—who is this?"

Rapper hung up.

So, Mr. Fenwood was calling his insurance agent about the stolen autocomms to get his insurance money for them. *There's no crime in that,* Rapper thought. Rapper could feel the presence of the tall, metal cabinet behind him. He knew he had to know what was inside. Rapper reached under the chair and pulled out the key. He inserted it into the lock and turned. It popped open. Rapper opened the cabinet.

From top to bottom, it was filled with papers and office supplies. Folders, pens, electronic notepads, disks. On the top shelf sat a nondescript, gray box. Rapper pulled it down. He flipped open the top flaps and looked inside.

Autocomms. Nine of them.

"I thought these were supposed to be stolen," Rapper said aloud.

Then the Holy Spirit softly spoke to Rapper's spirit. *They are stolen,* He said. *He's stealing them from himself.* Rapper closed the box and replaced it on the top shelf.

He's stealing them from himself. The words echoed in Rapper's spirit. Mr. Fenwood—who used to be a great man of faith—is taking autocomms from his own business, hiding them and then reporting them stolen? For insurance money?

Rapper could feel his mouth go dry. His stomach felt hollow. Mr. Fenwood gave up his relationship with the Lord for money. It was the cares of life, pulling his focus off what really mattered. It was *things.* That's what 2 Timothy 2:4 said. That was the truth. He got entangled in the cares of the world. Money had become his god. Even though Fenwood knew God alone gave the power to get wealth, God was no longer Fenwood's source. A fraudulent paycheck from an insurance agency was.

Rapper locked up the cabinet. As he replaced the key, his gaze focused on the picture of Karla on her father's desk. The heart around her face was simple and loving...and trusting. And her father had betrayed her. He was committing a crime. How could he do that? If anyone ever found out, he would go to jail. She would be without a father...without a family. All because of the cares of this world. All because of the love of money. All because of the love of *things.*

Rapper rubbed his eyes. *He* was the one who had found out, and he knew he had to tell someone. But what would that do to Karla? He couldn't leave her without a father. Rapper made his way out of the room, praying an easy answer would drop into his lap. It didn't happen.

Rapper replayed the facts in his mind. Maybe he had missed something. Maybe he was wrong about everything. That's it—a big misunderstanding. If only that were true.

It just made too much sense. Karla's dad hired two goons to break in on a regular basis—on the dates circled on his calendar. He provided them with the code to the front gate. They sneaked around the yard, dismantled autocomms from selected cars and then put them in Fenwood's very own hiding place. The next day, he would enter his office and count the autocomms they stole for him. Then Fenwood called Hank the insurance man and reported the autocomms stolen. Next, all he had to do was wait until the 30th of the month for his paycheck.

The pieces just fit into place. Buddy and Zeke and Karla probably had no clue. Of course, that still didn't explain Karla's strange behavior...unless she knew her dad had done some of these things. And, even more curious, how in the world were the robbers getting past the dogs?

Rapper scratched his head as he walked up the back stairs to the house. Maybe there was something more.

Maybe not. Regardless, Rapper knew he had to do something. He had to tell somebody. Not because he wanted to, but because it was the right thing to do. He decided to play it cool until he regrouped with Commander Kellie. He didn't need any trouble here.

The kitchen door slid open and Rapper stopped in his tracks when he saw Mr. Fenwood sitting at the table. Rapper could feel the color drain from his face.

Karla's dad stopped midbite and squinted at Rapper. He slapped his soup spoon down on the table like Karla had that morning. "Ugh! You still here?!"

Rapper put out his hands. He refused to get offended and stop the blessings of God from reaching him. In a way, that's how this all started in the first place. Back at Superkid Academy, when Mashela Knavery, the NME operative, was in custody, Rapper's friend Missy had gotten offended by some things Mashela had said. That offense, lodging in her heart, stifled God's blessings for her and things had turned topsy-turvy.

The next thing Rapper knew, Mashela had broken out, caught him and was off...only to drop him here. He'd had to fight against getting offended at her actions, too. But then again, she was only acting the way she'd been taught by NME. Rapper thanked God his friend Paul had shared the Word with her. Perhaps that Word in her heart would take root and soften her. Meanwhile, Rapper realized the sin of offense was something each of the Superkids had to battle at one time or another. Today, in Mr. Fenwood's kitchen, it was Rapper's turn.

"I'm just going to get my clothes," Rapper rapped, "and then I'll call for pick up, I suppose." Rapper found it hard to look the guilty man in the eye.

"Cute," Mr. Fenwood stated. "Well, the washer's that way." He pointed at the door Rapper just passed through.

Rapper nodded. He didn't say another word, but turned around and passed back out the door. He walked down to the garage. Through the garage, he found the laundry room again. He opened the washer and pulled out his uniform. He could feel his blood begin to boil. It was still soaked.

Rapper kicked the machine.

"Hey!"

Rapper spun around, surprised to see Mr. Fenwood on his way down the steps. Fenwood walked halfway into the garage and stared at the Superkid. "You always kick people's personal property?"

Rapper closed his eyes reminding himself that Proverbs 15:1 says a gentle answer turns away wrath. "I apologize. It's broken," he explained. "My uniform's still wet."

Fenwood shook his head. "Have you put it in the dryer?"

"It's been in there all morning," Rapper said coolly.

"No, it's been in the *washer* all morning. Now you have to dry it." Fenwood angled a finger at another unit a few feet away. Rapper blinked noticeably when he saw it.

"You mean you have to wash and dry in two *different* machines?" the Superkid asked. "That's like, ancient technology."

"It's what we can afford," Fenwood said with a mocking smirk. He turned around and headed away.

Rapper wanted to spurt out something about how he could afford more than that—Rapper knew—because he had all sorts of illegal money to use. But he reconsidered. He'd wait until he talked with Commander Kellie.

The Superkid loaded his uniform in the dryer and started it up. What next? Would his outfit shrink or something? What else could happen? How much longer did he have to wear the silly bow-covered candy canes? Rapper slapped the wall. Now he was stuck there until his clothes dried. Rapper turned the drying temperature up. Hopefully it wouldn't take long.

▲　▲　▲

Rapper made a brief call to Commander Kellie, letting her know that he was fine, but his outfit wasn't dry yet. He told her he'd call when it was ready. Commander Kellie offered to bring him a change of clothes, but Rapper said it would only be a short while. He had much more to tell her, but it could wait.

Meanwhile, as his clothes spun around the dryer, Rapper walked through the empty Fenwood household. Karla still had a few hours before school was out. Mr. Fenwood had retreated to his office. Buddy and Zeke were busy on-site.

Rapper went into his room and straightened up his bed, even though it didn't need straightening. He wiped off the mirror with his thick shirt sleeve. He squashed a menacing bug by the baseboard. He tossed his Superkid wings pin in the air and caught it time and again. He placed it onto the table by the bed.

As Rapper gazed around the room, he noticed there were simply no pictures around. He wondered if the bedroom had ever been used. His thoughts drifted to the two pictures he had seen around the property: the one of young Karla on her dad's desk and the one Karla had drawn in her room.

The Superkid got up and walked to Karla's room. Her door was open so he entered. He wasn't about to snoop, but he did look around. Maybe if he could find that Bible, he could read the Word for a while and strengthen his spirit. But it was out of plain sight.

Rapper noticed the picture was gone, too. Out of sight, out of mind, right? Rapper strolled over to Karla's window and looked out. A heap of trash was stacked along the side of the house. The longer Rapper peered at the trash, the more it looked like it wasn't there by accident. Rapper could almost make out a stair-step pattern on the heap.

The Superkid slid open the window. A cool breeze blew in, jogging Rapper's memory. He remembered how cool and crisp Karla's room had felt the night before. And the thumping sound—that could have been her window opening or closing. But why did Karla bother to open her window? It wasn't like the house was too hot or anything...

As Rapper slid the window shut, the sunlight bounced off the glass. It highlighted a small circle. A fingerprint. Rapper touched it. It didn't smudge. It was on the outside of the glass.

Rapper looked at the trash heap again. It *was* shaped like stair steps. Rapper gulped. He was wrong about one thing. Karla *did* know about her dad's business. She was helping out. She was sneaking out to calm the dogs while the thieves entered. *That's* why the dogs didn't bark. *Karla was in on it.*

▲   ▲   ▲

Shhhhhhhhooooommmm! When the back door leading into the kitchen slid back, Karla screamed. Rapper was sitting in one of the kitchen chairs, looking rather regal in his royal blue Superkid uniform, his feet propped up on the table. His brown eyes pierced her brown eyes. She jumped back.

"Y-you're still here?" Karla stuttered. She looked behind him, scanning the living room and hall.

"He's been working in the warehouse all afternoon," Rapper said, answering her obvious question.

"Why are you still here?" she asked, not moving.

Rapper didn't budge.

Karla looked down. "Why are you looking at me like that?"

"I want to know what's going on," Rapper demanded, taking his feet off the table.

"Rapper, I—"

"No. I want to know. I keep telling myself there must be some logical, innocent explanation for what I've discovered, but I'm not seeing it. I want to know how you can do this."

Karla tightened her thin lips and barreled past Rapper, heading toward her room. "I don't know what you're talking about."

"You don't know what I'm talking about?"

"No, I don't." Karla said, stopping abruptly. She tossed her book bag toward her room. It hit the door, near the bottom. She spun around and put her hands on her hips. "I don't know what you're talking about."

"I saw fingerprints on your bedroom window, Karla," Rapper let her know.

"What?!"

"And they were on the *outside.*" He said, "I know what's going on, so you don't have to hide it. I know you've been letting the Vipers in."

Karla walked back into the kitchen, plopped into one of the metal chairs and folded her arms across her chest. "This is none of your business."

"It's *illegal,* Karla."

"You don't think I know that?!"

"Then why do it?!"

"What am *I* doing?!" Karla exclaimed. "I'm not the one in the wrong!" Karla stomped the floor with her foot. "Look," she said softly, "I'm sorry. You shouldn't have gotten into this. It's not your business."

"Karla," Rapper pleaded, spinning his chair around and sitting in it backward, "you *brought* me into this. I was ready to go home. You insisted I stay. Why do you think that is?"

Karla fidgeted with her hands. "I don't know. I don't...Rapper, you have to understand. This could ruin our family. It's really not your business."

"Like it or not," Rapper explained, "it is my business now. I've figured out what's going on, Karla. And I have to tell the authorities. I don't want to, but it's not right *not* to. Please—let me help."

Karla buried her face in her hands. Rapper could see the stress on her forehead. "My mom isn't going to take this well," Karla murmured.

Rapper was about to console Karla when suddenly his ears perked up. He leaned toward her. His mouth was gaping, but he didn't care. "Did you just say your *mom* won't take this well?"

Karla slid a finger aside and peeked an eye out at Rapper. "You *don't* know what's going on, do you?"

Rapper's mind reeled. His jaw moved up and down, but no words came out. Finally he said, "Maybe I...don't."

Karla pulled her hands down her face and then stood up. She paced the room as Rapper sat stunned, thoughts racing through his mind. Her *mom?*

Karla walked over and pushed the button by the back door. Rapper heard it lock.

"Rapper, you were partly right," Karla admitted. "I have been letting the Vipers in. I've been letting them into my room. But they're not Vipers. They're my parents."

"Whoa-whoa," Rapper said, popping out of his seat. "Are you telling me your parents are Vipers?!"

"No, I'm telling you the Vipers are my parents."

"But they're not Vipers."

"No. They're my parents."

Rapper's forehead wrinkled as his right eyebrow lifted. "So...who's the guy you keep calling 'Dad?'"

Karla chuckled uncomfortably. "Maybe you haven't noticed, but I've never called him my dad—you have."

"You never told me he *wasn't* your dad."

"I never told you he *was.*"

Rapper found himself blinking a lot as the strong revelations hit him like baseballs to his skull.

Rapper threw his hands up in the air. "You're right— I don't get it."

"That's fine," Karla said, waving her hand aside. "The less you know, the better. You don't have to meddle, Rapper. I don't want to lose my family."

Rapper slowly stood up and peered out the kitchen window. He looked at the trash raised along the side of the house. He glanced from it to Karla. He repeated her words, "I don't want to lose my family."

Karla nodded.

Rapper looked outside again. "When I was 6, my parents divorced. When I was 8, my big brother was killed in a gang shooting. Now, I'm happy if I see my dad for Christmas—you know, if he's not too busy. And for years, I've thought no one else had it worse than me family-wise."

Karla stopped pacing.

"But this tops it all," Rapper stated. "You're living with some guy who's—what? Your *kidnapper?* Is that why you only get to see your parents when you sneak them in at night?"

"It gets worse," Karla whispered.

"You're telling me!" Rapper exclaimed. "Because then you—living like this—tell me that anything I might do to help could *ruin* your family! What kind of family *is* this?!"

Karla hardened her eyes on Rapper. "It's the only family I've got," she resolved. A sudden tear crept down her cheek. She quickly wiped it away. Rapper felt his heart melt. He apologized. Karla shook her head.

"Let me put things into perspective," she said. "First of all, I don't *want* things this way. But this is how they are."

Rapper stayed silent.

"My parents told me that just before I was born, NME took an interest in some of the electronics my dad could get here at the junkyard. They wanted them—especially autocomms, because he could salvage them for a low price."

Rapper shook his head. *Why doesn't it surprise me that NME is somehow involved in this?* he thought.

"But, Rapper, my dad is a man of honor. God was blessing him and he refused to sell *anything* to NME."

"Your dad stood up to NME?" Rapper asked. The thought brought a light smile to Rapper's face.

Karla looked at the floor. "He did...but the stress was intense—especially for my mom. The doctors said it was a miracle I lived at birth.

"That was 12 years ago. My dad resisted for about a year and a half after that. Then, NME barged in one night and took over. They took my 4-year-old sister, Jaqi, to insure that my dad would do what they wanted. Then they placed their own agent in control of my dad's junkyard."

Rapper pointed to the back door.

"That's right," Karla said. "It's the guy you keep calling my dad. That NME agent assumed my dad's identity, 'Kentren Fenwood III.' He hired new employees, Buddy and Zeke, and ran this junkyard as a front to supply NME with autocomms."

"That's when your dad stopped ministering to the Vipers," Rapper concluded. "He...didn't have a choice."

"Rapper, it broke his heart, but he didn't know what to do. NME keeps my parents around because my dad's an expert at extracting autocomms. But they told my parents that if they said anything to anyone or tried to run with me, they'd never see Jaqi again."

"So NME kidnapped Jaqi and kept you *here* as ransom—to keep your parents in their service."

Karla bit her lip. "My parents don't serve NME," she stated. "They're slaves."

Rapper wanted to say he was sorry again, but the words seemed trite compared to what Karla shouldered.

"So where do your parents live?" the Superkid asked.

Karla shook her head. "For the first five years, the agent allowed my parents to stay in your room, posing as my aunt and uncle. I think he did it so he'd have help raising me. But when I was seven, he kicked them out and ordered them to do their work at night. They couldn't visit me any more. I don't know why, but they had to sneak in using his security code, dressed as Vipers. To this day, that's how they come in to work. They extract autocomms and deliver them to his office.

Then he sells them to NME. They live at a homeless shelter in town now."

Karla smiled. "That NME agent still thinks I believe he's my father, but I know better. I sneak my parents into my room at night. I have for years. And he's clueless."

"Except for the fact that you're always tired," Rapper interjected. Then he added, "So he's got your parents *stealing* the autocomms?"

Karla shook her head. "No, they just deliver them to the agent's office. I don't know who's stealing them."

Rapper figured it out. The fact was, no one was stealing them. The NME agent was just *reporting* them stolen. And, of course, he never shared this with Karla.

"We've been praying for help," Karla mentioned. "I guess that's why I wanted you to stay. Since you're a Superkid, I thought you might be the help we were praying for."

"It's been 10 years," Rapper said. "You've been praying for *10* years...and you never gave up?"

"My dad is who you said he is," Karla confirmed. "He is a man of God. He has taught me God's Word. He has never lost his faith. He showed me 2 Corinthians 4:18 and told me I can believe by faith for things I can't see."

"And you never doubted?"

"Like Romans 4:21 says, we are fully persuaded that God has the power to do what He promised."

Rapper felt a sudden surge of joy well up inside him—the real Kentren Fenwood III *hadn't* given up. *He hadn't given up his relationship with the Lord for things!* Rapper walked over, pulled his friend out of her chair and gave her a hug. "God did send me to help you," he said. "I'm going to get you out of this."

"Are you sure?" Karla asked, with a faint smile. Rapper nodded.

"All right," she agreed. "But please be careful. I don't want to lose my parents if NME finds out."

"You won't," Rapper assured her, heading for the ComPhone. His mind went back to Karla's drawing of the house with bars over the door. "We're going to get you out of this jail. I promise."

Dinner at the Fenwood household was quiet, but back to normal. The agent who called himself Kentren Fenwood was pleased about that. Finally, the menacing Superkid was out of his and Karla's lives, hopefully never to be seen again. He figured he gave Rapper a good enough scare. It was worth it to stop him from meddling. Last thing he needed was Karla becoming friends with someone like that.

He tried making conversation with the preteen time and again, but his questions fell on seemingly deaf ears. She answered him with "uh-huh's" and "yeah's" and grunts, but no real conversation flourished.

"I'm sorry it didn't work out with your friend," the man said softly. "But look at the bright side: He wasn't the best influence anyway."

"Yeah," Karla said sadly.

The agent put down his silverware. The reheated chicken-fried steak, gravy-covered mashed potatoes and peas didn't look so appetizing anymore. It broke his heart to hurt Karla by running her friend away. Rapper was her first friend in a long while...but he didn't see any other way to quickly handle the problem. Running the Superkid off was something he had to do...if he and Karla were to stay together.

"I'm sorry," he said after clearing his throat. "You know I love you, don't you?"

Karla gazed across the table at him, but didn't say a word.

▲　▲　▲

Inside, Karla felt butterflies. Unknown to the man who sat across from her—the man who said he was her father—she knew tonight was the night. Things were going to change for better or for worse. She prayed to God they would change for the better...she had to leave everything in His capable hands now.

When the man asked her if she knew he loved her, she didn't answer. She couldn't answer. How could he love her and do this to her? How could he keep her trapped in a prison all her life? Well, tonight the truth would be known. He thought he had run Rapper off...but...

Karla heard a rock hit the windowpane. That was her cue. She placed her hand on her knee to keep her leg from jumping. She turned slightly in her chair.

"Did you hear something outside?" she asked.

▲　▲　▲

The agent's eyebrows shot up. He hadn't heard anything. Why was Karla trying to change the subject?

Why didn't she answer his question? Did she doubt that he loved her? How could she doubt that? He had become her father...and he tried to be the best father he could be. He didn't mean for it to happen this way...it just did. One moment he was just an NME agent trying to climb higher in the ranks. The next moment, in a new assignment, he was forced to play house and be a little girl's father. He hated it at the time. But now...

Karla was staring back at the door.

"I'm sure I heard a noise," she said.

The agent glanced down at his food. He never should have let that Superkid stay in his house.

Suddenly the dogs started barking. The agent stiffened in his chair. Now *that* was unusual. He narrowed his eyes, looking at Karla. Perhaps she was right. There was someone out there who wasn't supposed to be. Could it be for once that they really *did* have thieves prowling the yard?

Pushing his chair back, the man stood up. He pulled his laser rifle out of the long, vertical cabinet. Karla seemed concerned when he grabbed it, but he knew it may be necessary. He slid the back door open. He didn't want to come barreling out the front—he would lose the element of surprise.

He slowly walked down the stairs with Karla only steps behind him. At the bottom of the stairs, he froze. He heard something. Rocks shifting...junk clinking...

something. He looked in the direction of the sound. He raised his weapon.

▲   ▲   ▲

Rapper, standing behind a mountain of junk, closed his eyes, said a quick prayer and let out a long breath. This was it. He jumped out. The rapid charging of the laser rifle echoed in Rapper's ears as he shouted, "Yo! It's me!"

Not a second too soon, Mr. Fenwood released his finger from the trigger. He squinted at Rapper. His graying brows furrowed. "What are *you* still doing here?!" he shouted angrily. Rapper glanced back at Karla, standing behind Fenwood. She watched without a word, her brown eyes wide.

The man stomped forward, demanding to know why Rapper was still on his property. He grabbed Rapper's arm and shook him. Rapper struggled out of his grasp.

"I've caught the robbers!" Rapper announced. He brushed the wrinkled sleeve of his royal blue Superkid uniform.

"You *what?!*" Fenwood demanded.

"I caught the thieves—the Vipers!" Rapper said. "I told you God would bring things to light! They won't be stealing from you anymore!"

Karla jumped in excitement, grabbing the agent's arm. "You caught—he caught the thieves!"

The agent was stunned, unsure what to say.

"Don't you want to see them?" Rapper asked.

The agent jolted out of his stupor and looked at Karla. "I...of course I do...uh...good job..." He dropped the laser weapon to his side. "Karla, honey, why don't you go back into the house. It's safer there."

Karla glanced at Rapper, and then agreed. She made her way inside.

"C'mon!" Rapper said, excited. "You're going to love this!" He started to jog away.

"Where are they?" the agent asked. Rapper didn't answer, but kept moving. He didn't want to lose the momentum of the moment.

The agent soon picked up his pace and followed the Superkid past a few junk piles, then past his workers' booths. Finally, he realized Rapper was headed toward the warehouse. He followed along warily, but obediently.

Rapper was particularly pleased by the ominous screeching the old-fashioned warehouse door made when opening. He knew it sent a shiver down the agent's spine. The truth has a way of doing that.

When they entered the small office, the agent froze. He stared over at his desk. Behind it, tied from torso to hip in thick rope sat the two masked Vipers. They sat still, not saying a word. The agent himself was speechless.

Rapper took the moment to embellish. "They were really quite easy to catch," he said. "Once I learned their MO—their 'mode of operation'—I just put myself in the right place at the right time."

The agent didn't say a word.

Rapper walked up to the Vipers and walked behind them. "Now to see who our Viper impostors really are!" At once, he yanked the black mask off each Viper. The man and woman both had black hair and brown eyes. The woman's skin was a bit lighter, and her face longer. Neither were smiling. They looked at the agent in surprise.

The agent calling himself Fenwood turned his head when the voice behind him gasped, "It's my aunt and uncle!" Karla had entered the room and appeared genuinely surprised.

The agent shook his head nervously. He looked at the man and woman tied up before him. "I...I can't believe it," he said softly. "Who'd have guessed?!" He smiled.

Rapper walked to the side of the captured Vipers and straightened the ComPhone on the desk with a tap. "Should we call the authorities?!" he asked, his fingers hovering over the ComPhone.

The agent hesitated.

"No," Rapper said boldly, catching him off guard. "You don't want to do that, do you?"

The agent shot his gaze at Rapper.

The Superkid continued, "No...if you call the authorities, they'll arrest these 'impostors.' But you don't want to lose your thieves...because then you'll lose the insurance money you're collecting from the autocomms you force them to steal."

The agent narrowed his eyes. He quickened. "You accusing me of something?" he demanded, his hand tightening around the laser rifle. "I don't know what you're talking about. I'm not the one causing trouble here—these two are." He pointed at the fake Vipers. "They're the ones who have stolen my autocomms. I even had nine stolen last night!"

Rapper bent down and reached under the rolling chair. He removed the silver key and popped open the lock.

"Hey! What are you doing?!" the agent shouted, but he didn't move.

Rapper shoved open the metal cabinet's doors and pulled down the box on the top shelf. One by one, he removed the autocomms until nine sat on the desk.

"You're right," Rapper said to him. "There were nine."

The agent cast a glance back at Karla, then raised his weapon at Rapper. "So what?" he demanded. "With you out of the way, who will know?"

"All this time I thought you had let the devil squeeze God's Word out of you," Rapper said. "Truth is, you never had it in you in the first place."

The agent peered into the weapon's viewfinder.

Karla tugged on the agent's sleeve. "Dad," she asked, playing along, "what are you doing?!"

"You're too young to understand all this," he threw at her, sounding a bit sad. "But everything will be all right. Daddy did this because he cares about you, Karla. Don't forget that. I love you."

Karla nodded her head. "No, I understand. *Love.* Love is the reason you've tried to keep my parents from me all these years."

Rapper felt the ping of pain in his heart as the agent heard the girl call his bluff. As his face dropped, he suddenly looked older. The agent lowered his weapon.

"But I...I'm your parent," he insisted. "I'm your dad."

The male Viper stared straight ahead at the agent and explained with two simple words: "She knows."

By the look on the agent's face, Rapper could see his anger rising, his heartbeat quickening, his body flooding with adrenaline.

"This has to stop!" the agent cried. "It's madness!" He turned to Karla, who was backing away. "Don't be afraid, Karla—I'll make things right."

He raised the laser rifle again. He punched a button on the side, flooding it with full power.

"Explain the truth to Karla," he demanded of the real Mr. and Mrs. Fenwood. "Explain it the way we talked about!"

"Or what?" Mr. Fenwood asked.

"Or"—he nodded to Karla—"I'll make a call and you'll never see her or your other daughter again."

Mr. and Mrs. Fenwood's eyebrows wrinkled. Mrs. Fenwood bit her bottom lip and looked down.

Rapper moved to the side of the desk. "That's an empty threat," he announced. Mr. and Mrs. Fenwood looked up. The agent looked at Rapper, questioning.

"I phoned Superkid Academy today," Rapper explained. "Commander Kellie did some research, and do you know what she found out?"

The room was silent, save the buzzing of the laser rifle.

"NME dropped this project five years ago," he said. "That's about the time you forced Mr. and Mrs. Fenwood to start acting like Vipers. The truth is, this NME agent has lied to you more than you think. The force of NME is no longer behind him...they dropped this project like a lead balloon. This fake no longer has any control over Karla...or any influence with NME where Jaqi is concerned."

Rapper lowered his voice and searched the ex-NME agent's brown eyes. "You could have left with NME and given this family their lives back. Why? Why did you stay?"

The agent swallowed hard. "I couldn't leave Karla," he said hoarsely. "She became like my own daughter. I couldn't give her up." Somehow Rapper understood... the agent had never known love, and this was the closest thing to it he'd ever experienced. Even though it was built on a lie.

To the agent's surprise, Mr. Fenwood stood up, the ropes around him falling off. They were never really tied in the first place. "Karla wasn't yours to take!" he shouted, his eyes flashing. "She is *our* daughter!"

"Back off!" the agent shouted.

Karla's father pushed the desk and it skidded forward a foot. The small picture of Karla toppled off and hit the ground, the glass shattering. "You kept my daughter from me all this time?!!"

The agent stepped back in fear and pulled the trigger on his buzzing weapon.

Click.

The agent's mouth dropped. He pulled the trigger twice more.

Click. Click.

Rapper held his hand out before him. "This would help," Rapper said. There, in his palm, he held the gun's laser filament. Without it, the gun was useless. "If you had this, you could shoot a bolt of lightning at me again, like you did when we first met and you tried to keep me from figuring out your plan."

The agent threw his weapon on the cement. It hit with a crash.

"You won't live through the night!" he cried, shoving his finger forward angrily.

Rapper grabbed the ComPhone and spun it around. The bearded face on the viewer stared forward at the agent.

"You get all that, Hank?" Rapper asked the Insurecom Insurance agent.

Hank's face smiled at the NME agent. "Yep," he said. "I'm a witness to insurance fraud, kidnapping, attempted murder... The authorities are on their way as we speak."

"It's amazing how things fall apart when you're out of God's will," Rapper said.

"And how they come together when you're in it," the real Kentren Fenwood added.

Breaking out in a sweat and full of fury, the NME agent ran out of the warehouse. The old-fashioned door smashed open and slammed shut. Rapper took off after him, not wasting a moment.

"Be careful, Rapper!" Karla shouted.

Outside, Rapper spun on his heels and looked for the agent. There! Rapper saw him round the corner at the side of the house. Rapper ran after him, his heart beating rapidly.

"Spread Your protection over me, Lord," Rapper said aloud, encouraging himself with Psalm 5:11.

As he rounded the corner, he saw the agent dive behind a mountain of garbage. Rapper ran up to the pile and listened. He didn't hear the agent running ahead. Rapper knew he was around the corner.

Whap! Rapper fell to the ground as the NME agent broke an old board across his back. Rapper rolled over and saw the agent standing above him. Using a maneuver he'd learned in his gang days, Rapper flipped his body up in a swift movement, placing him back on his feet.

"Why couldn't you just leave well enough alone?" the agent shouted, grabbing an electronic unit of some kind from the pile. He tossed it at Rapper, but the Superkid dodged it.

"I didn't see that things were well enough," Rapper replied curtly. "Give yourself up—it'll be better for you."

"What do I have to lose?" the agent asked. "You've already taken everything I loved away from me!"

Rapper dodged a hovercar engine component the agent hurled at him.

"I didn't take anything you truly owned away," Rapper argued. "The truth is, all you had was a lie."

The junkyard dogs started barking.

The agent grabbed a steel beam from the trash heap and held it over his head. Rapper ran farther into the maze of junk. The agent followed closely, swinging the beam at Rapper every chance he had.

Crunch! The beam hit a trash pile, scattering debris everywhere. Rapper shielded his eyes and dove to the ground.

The agent stepped forward, confident. He came down at Rapper with the beam as though he were chopping wood with an ax.

Thump! The beam hit the ground as Rapper rolled aside. A large gash was left in the clay.

"You don't want to do this!" Rapper cried.

"You ruined my life!" the agent shouted.

Thump! The beam came down on the other side of Rapper. He scurried back on his hands and feet like a crab. He stood up. The agent came at Rapper with full force. Rapper turned to run—and ran right into a junked hovercar. He rolled onto the hood.

The agent came down with the steel beam, shattering the windshield as Rapper slid aside. Suddenly Rapper felt his breath cut short—he was out of places to run. He was stuck in a notch of the trash heap.

The NME agent raised the steel beam.

Rapper shouted, "Jesus!"

Suddenly, like a canister in a vacuum chute, the agent shot straight up. Rapper's eyes widened as the man was lifted 100 feet into the air, as if God were holding the other end of the steel beam between His thumb and forefinger.

Rapper gazed into the distance and he saw Karla waving at him...from Buddy's raised booth. She was operating the hovering electromagnetic disc...the disc that had the NME agent up in the air, holding onto the steel beam for dear life.

"Once again, thank You, Jesus," Rapper whispered. He dropped his head back on the hood of the old hovercar and let out a long breath. Above him, the agent shouted curses. And in the distance, Rapper heard approaching sirens.

The humbled ex-NME agent ducked his head as the law officer pushed him into the back seat of the hovercar. He was handcuffed now. Rapper watched the red, blue and green lights of the law pass across the impostor's countenance. He looked sad, beaten and regretful. He'd let the enemy lead him astray...and he'd kept going until he hit a brick wall—the Truth—that shot him back into reality.

The real Kentren Fenwood interrupted Rapper's thoughts when he put an arm around the Superkid's shoulders and shook his hand.

"Thank you," he said, simply. Rapper nodded.

They stood there for a long while, watching, while the officers questioned the crowd. Hank the Insurecom Insurance agent had arrived. Buddy and Zeke were close behind. Commander Kellie had come, too, and was talking with Karla now.

"So how'd you do it?" Rapper asked Karla's real dad.

"Do what?"

"You know," Rapper said, "go on year after year, just waiting."

"I never let go of God's promise," Mr. Fenwood explained. "Second Timothy 3:14 says to continue to hold onto what we have learned. I never let God's promises go. The enemy attacked, but I knew God would show Himself strong on my behalf. I just had to remain faithful. And I know that even though NME has our daughter Jaqi somewhere, God will find a way for her to return to us as well."

Rapper allowed the words to sink into his heart. Mr. Fenwood never let go. He remained faithful. The statements were like fountains of refreshment to Rapper. Each word felt like cool rain on his spirit. Kentren Fenwood III hadn't lost his faith. He hadn't been led astray. Rapper wasn't sure why it was so thrilling to know that...but somehow it meant so much to him.

Leaving Rapper's side, Mr. Fenwood joined his wife. Karla joined them both and gave them the first hug she ever remembered giving them in freedom. From the hovercar, the NME agent watched. When Karla let go, she slowly approached the hovercar. The back door was still open. Karla reached inside and, to Rapper's surprise, she hugged the agent.

"I'm just getting what I gave for so many years," the agent whispered to her. His voice was still hoarse. "I forced your parents to visits only...now *I'm* forced to visits only. You will visit me, won't you?"

Karla nodded and wiped a tear out of the corner of her eye.

"I'm sorry. I really do love you," the agent told her softly.

"I know," Karla replied. She reached into her pocket and pulled out her tattered, blue, pocket Bible. She handed it to him.

"Read this," she said. "I want you to find out what a father's love is supposed to be."

The agent smiled weakly as she tucked the gift into the front pocket of his overalls. He leaned forward and kissed Karla on the cheek. She hugged him one more time.

Shortly, a law officer shut the hovercar door and, with a rush of air, the hovercars drove off.

Karla joined Rapper, Commander Kellie, Buddy, Zeke, Hank and her parents again.

"Well the good news," Commander Kellie explained, "is that this yard is still in the name of Kentren Fenwood III. Mr. Fenwood, this is all yours. Every bit of work that has been done over the past 10 years is yours to reap."

"And," Hank added, "there's a hefty amount of extra wealth that NME officer scammed off us to build this place up. It's in the equipment, the security system and the buildings. It's all yours."

"I don't have to pay it back?" Mr. Fenwood questioned.

The insurance agent shook his head. "We'll get our money," he promised, "but not from you. It's the NME agent...er, ex-NME agent, who's going to be paying back every cent. You can count on that."

Kentren Fenwood tightened his hug-hold on his wife and daughter.

"Uh, sir?" Buddy asked. "We'd love to continue working for you, sir. We didn't know nothing about all this, I assure you."

"I believe you," Mr. Fenwood said. He shook Buddy's hand. "It's a deal then."

Zeke squealed with delight. It made everybody laugh.

A long pause followed and then Karla tapped Rapper on the arm.

"Looks like your uniform needs a good wash, Superkid," she said.

Rapper threw up his hands and stepped back. "No way!" he jeered. "I'm wearing this thing until we get back to the Academy and I can change into some of my *own* clothes. No offense."

Karla giggled. "None taken."

"Where are your wings?" Commander Kellie asked. Rapper looked down, his chin hitting the collar of his uniform.

"Guess I forgot to put them on," he said. "They're probably still in the house. I'll be right back."

As each of Rapper's friends, old and new, parted ways, Rapper ran up the winding, creaking, wooden steps of the bi-level house one more time. He went down the hall, into his temporary room and, sure enough, his wings were still sitting on the table by the bed. As he pinned them to his uniform, he slowly looked around the room...the simple bed, the end table, the small window. Just as he turned to look in the mirror, he heard Karla and her parents enter the house.

Rapper stopped his gaze short and shut off the light. He had taken in enough. The room belonged to someone else now, as did the memories, which the walls held in silence. He didn't have to look in the mirror and wonder if he would ever give up his faith. He knew the answer: As long as he kept the Word in his heart and kept his relationship with the Lord strong, the things of the world just wouldn't have their appeal. It would be a daily walk, a daily faith, but—with the Anointed One in him—he could, like Kentren Fenwood III, make it through anything.

Rapper waved goodbye to the Fenwoods and headed out the door...back to the life he loved, back to his life at Superkid Academy.

As Rapper left behind the junkyard mystery, he also, unknown to him, left behind one clue he was never to discover.

It was the one clue that revealed he hadn't been dropped into the junkyard by accident.

It was the one clue that implied he had been watched during his entire adventure.

It was the one clue that suggested Karla's sister, Jaqi, knew she had been stolen by NME for their service...

...and that she would, one day, in her own time, reunite with her parents.

The clue was a short message, written in black marker, on the mirror in Rapper's temporary room.

It was a message that simply read, "Thank you. Mashela."

With the hardest days of the year behind them, Paul, Missy and Rapper took off for Christmas vacation. Valerie and Alex's vacations were scheduled to start a couple days after the others, as they had to wait for transportation. For Alex, it was a bit of a downer, but Valerie was used to it. Her parents lived on Calypso Island in the South Pacific and easy transportation was always a challenge.

Since she and Alex were the two highest-trained Superkids left at the Academy, it came as no surprise to Valerie when Commander Kellie called them in for a meeting.

"Three months," Commander Kellie was saying, holding up three fingers. "In three months we've lost three aircraft over the Pacific Ocean. And all three were lost in the same general area. We want to know why."

"What happened to the pilots?" Alex wondered.

Commander Kellie brushed a strand of hair behind her right ear. "They're fine—when their ships' systems mysteriously died, they ejected. But the 'Copters sank. And when we swept the ocean floor for them, we found no evidence they were ever there in the first place."

"They disappeared?" Valerie asked.

"They disappeared."

"And you want *us* to go look for them?" Alex inquired.

"I do," the commander confirmed.

"We can do it," Valerie said with a smile. Her stomach tightened a little as her mind added, *I hope!*

Alex asked, "How do we know Val and I won't disappear, too?"

Commander Kellie smiled. "We're equipping you with"—Commander Kellie held up two fingers—"*two* SuperCopters that have multiple safety measures. You'll have complete backup engine systems, long-range scanners and, if all else fails, ejectable pilot seats.

"Plus," Commander Kellie added, "we're going to pray right now."

Valerie and Alex stood, following their commander's lead. They grabbed hands as Commander Kellie prayed. "Father God, I thank You for Your unfailing love toward us. I send Valerie and Alex out today to find the answers I know You want us to find. I assign angels to protect them according to Psalm 91:11, and we rejoice for Psalm 37:23 states that You order their steps. Because of Your protection, we believe that nothing—no evildoer, no work of the enemy, no shark—shall by any means hurt them…"

Valerie's right eye popped open. *Did she just say "shark?"*

To be continued...

Three ships have vanished into thin air.
Now it's up to Valerie to find them…
without becoming the **fourth.**

Look for *Commander Kellie and the Superkids*_{SM}
novel #7—

Out of Breath

by Christopher P.N. Maselli

Prayer for Salvation

Father God, I believe that Jesus is Your Son and that You raised Him from the dead for me. Jesus, I give my life to You. Right now, I make You the Lord of my life and choose to follow You forever. I love You and I know You love me. Thank You, Jesus, for giving me a new life. Thank You for coming into my heart and being my Savior. I am a child of God! Amen.

About the Author

Christopher P.N. Maselli is the author of the *Commander Kellie and the Superkids* Adventure Series. He also writes the bimonthly children's magazine, *Shout! The Voice of Victory for Kids,* and has contributed to the *Commander Kellie and the Superkids* movies.

Originally from Iowa and a graduate of Oral Roberts University, Chris now lives in Fort Worth, Texas, with his wife, Gena, where he is actively involved in the children's ministry at his local church. When he's not writing, he enjoys in-line skating, playing computer games and collecting Legos.

Other Books Available

Baby Praise Board Book
Baby Praise Christmas Board Book
Noah's Ark Coloring Book
The Best of *Shout!* Adventure Comics
The *Shout!* Joke Book
The *Shout!* Super-Activity Book

*Commander Kellie and the Superkids*_{SM} **Books:**

The SWORD Adventure Book
*Commander Kellie and the Superkids*_{SM} *Series*
    Middle Grade Novels by Christopher P.N. Maselli

    #1 *The Mysterious Presence*
    #2 *The Quest for the Second Half*
    #3 *Escape From Jungle Island*
    #4 *In Pursuit of the Enemy*
    #5 *Caged Rivalry*
    #6 *Mystery of the Missing Junk*

World Offices
of Kenneth Copeland Ministries

For more information about KCM and a free
catalog, please write the office nearest you:

Kenneth Copeland Ministries
Fort Worth, Texas 76192-0001

Kenneth Copeland
Locked Bag 2600
Mansfield Delivery Centre
QUEENSLAND 4122
AUSTRALIA

Kenneth Copeland
Post Office Box 15
BATH
BA1 3XN
ENGLAND U.K.

Kenneth Copeland
Private Bag X 909
FONTAINEBLEAU
2032
REPUBLIC OF SOUTH AFRICA

Kenneth Copeland
Post Office Box 378
Surrey
BRITISH COLUMBIA
V3T 5B6
CANADA

UKRAINE
L'VIV 290000
Post Office Box 84
Kenneth Copeland Ministries
L'VIV 290000
UKRAINE

JESUS IS LORD

We're Here for You!

Shout! ...The dynamic magazine just for kids!

Shout! The Voice of Victory for Kids is a Bible-charged, action-packed, bimonthly magazine available FREE to kids everywhere! Featuring *Wichita Slim* and *Commander Kellie and the Superkids, Shout!* is filled with colorful adventure comics, challenging games and puzzles, exciting short stories, solve-it-yourself mysteries and much more!!

Stand up, sign up and get ready to *Shout!*

Believer's Voice of Victory Television Broadcast

Join Kenneth and Gloria Copeland, and the *Believer's Voice of Victory* broadcasts, Monday through Friday and on Sunday each week, and learn how faith in God's Word can take your life from ordinary to extraordinary. This teaching from God's Word is designed to get you where you want to be—*on top!*

You can catch the *Believer's Voice of Victory* broadcast on your local, cable or satellite channels.

*Check your local listings for times and stations in your area.

Believer's Voice of Victory Magazine

Enjoy inspired teaching and encouragement from Kenneth and Gloria Copeland and guest ministers each month in the *Believer's Voice of Victory* magazine. Also included are real-life testimonies of God's miraculous power and divine intervention into the lives of people just like you!

It's more than just a magazine—it's a ministry.

If you or some of your friends would like to receive a FREE subscription to *Shout!,* just send each kid's name, date of birth and complete address to:

Kenneth Copeland Ministries
Fort Worth, Texas 76192-0001
Or call:
1-800-600-7395
(9 a.m.-5 p.m. CT)
Or log on to our Web site at:
www.kcm.org

The Harrison House Vision

Proclaiming the truth and the power
Of the Gospel of Jesus Christ
With excellence;

Challenging Christians to
Live victoriously,
Grow spiritually,
Know God intimately.